16

Tomás González

THE STORM

Translated from the Spanish
by Andrea Rosenberg

archipelago books

First Archipelago Books Edition, 2018

Library of Congress Cataloging-in-Publication Data
González, Tomás, (1950-) | Rosenberg, Andrea translator.
The Storm / Tomas Gonzalez ; translated from the Spanish by Andrea Rosenberg.
Other titles: Temporal. English
First Archipelago Books edition. | Archipelago Books : Brooklyn, NY, 2018.
LCCN 2018001760 (print) | LCCN 2018005916 (ebook)
ISBN 9781939810038 (el) | ISBN 9781939810021 (tr)
LCSH: Fathers and sons--Fiction. | Brothers--Fiction. | Family life--Fiction.
GSAFD: Domestic fiction | Psychological fiction
CC PQ8180.17.O483 (ebook) | LCC PQ8180.17.O483 T4613 2018 (print) | DDC 863/.64--dc23
LC record available at https://lccn.loc.gov/2018001760

Archipelago Books
232 3rd Street #A111
Brooklyn, NY 11215
www.archipelagobooks.org

Distributed by Penguin Random House
www.penguinrandomhouse.com

Cover art: Thomas Wågström

Translated with the support of the Banff International Literary Translation Centre (BILTC)
at The Banff Centre, Banff, Alberta, Canada.

This work was made possible by the New York State Council on the Arts with the support of
Governor Andrew M. Cuomo and the New York State Legislature.

Archipelago Books also gratefully acknowledges the generous support from Lannan Foundation,
the Carl Lesnor Family Foundation, the National Endowment for the Arts, and
the New York City Department of Cultural Affairs.

PRINTED IN CANADA

THE STORM

Elle est retrouvée.
Quoi ? – L'Eternité.
C'est la mer allée
Avec le soleil.

—Arthur Rimbaud

Raging, aimless wind
that sweeps away so many things
from this world,
carry off the anguish
of my sorrow,
which runs so deep.

—Javier Solís

Saturday, 4:00 a.m.

Angrily, but with great care, Mario placed two oars in the boat and went to his father's house to fetch the gas cans. Javier had already brought the coolers full of ice and the jugs of water, and by now he'd be back at his bungalow, boiling the breakfast eggs and pouring coffee into the thermoses. Mario had been born two hours after Javier and frequently wished he'd never been born at all. The thirty-foot motorboat was a sky-blue fiberglass craft, and a Coleman lantern glowed on one of the benches. Despite the chill at this early hour, Mario wasn't wearing a shirt. The heat of his resentment toward his father kept him warm enough.

Had he bothered to notice them, he'd have admired the net of stars stretching over the vault of the heavens. But though he looked up at the sky, he didn't see the stars or refused to see them. Javier knew about ursas major and minor and southern crosses; Mario was the one who could take an outboard motor apart and put it back together with his eyes closed and navigate the gulf even though he knew nothing about crosses. A bolt of lightning, its tentacles reaching down toward the horizon, caught his eye, and he also noted the absence of wind. His notice was not born of admiration, since he wasn't the sort to admire the shape of lightning or the wind or the absence of wind, but because he was alert to everything related to the sea and fishing.

The guest who'd been up drinking all night in the only bungalow besides Mario's that was lit up at this hour turned off his Carlos Gardel album and switched out the lights. Between Gardel, Olimpo Cárdenas, and the gale of resentment inside him, the twin hadn't been able to sleep much that night. The tourist's bungalow was only a few meters from his, and even though he didn't have the music turned up loud, it was still audible. But Mario wasn't upset about it; these disruptions were part of his job. The guests were paying to get drunk at the seaside, and that's how he made his living, how all of them did.

He went to the rear patio of his father's bungalow. The old man was currently a mile away, off the coast by the airport, pulling in bait with the cast net. Mario picked up two red gas cans and placed them in the prow of the boat. Then he went back for the other two. The insects flung themselves against the Coleman lantern, wheeled around it. The waves unfurled almost silently over the sand. By the bungalows, bats were flitting among the coconut palms and the almond trees, though neither Mario nor anyone else could see them at the moment. Maybe God was aware of them, but as far as Mario was concerned, God didn't exist.

They were preparing for a full day and night of fishing in a place some two hours out to sea, just beyond the mouth of the gulf. The plan was to bring in seven or eight hundred pounds of mojarras, blue runners, sea bass, crevalle jacks, Atlantic tarpons, lane snappers, and black margates, which the guests, perpetually ravenous thanks to either the sea air or their hangovers, would wolf down in the hotel restaurant with fried plantain, coconut rice, and tomato-and-onion salad, as they'd been doing during the high season, day after day, for many years.

Mario placed the other two gas cans in the boat and went to fetch the mangrove-wood pole that they used to push against the sandy bottom. Beside his bungalow was bungalow number two, where his mother had been talking to herself day after day, also for many years. The bungalows went from one to fifteen, with the numerals crudely painted in white on raw pieces of wood and mounted above the front doors. His was number three; his brother was in nine. The father's didn't have a number. Actually, Nora hadn't been talking to herself – she'd been talking to a large number of people, sometimes in a quiet voice, sometimes a little louder, but almost never shouting. Despite being a "total nutcase" – that's how the twins referred to her condition, though they loved their mother – she was lucid enough to realize that her husband might come and shut her up.

Mario took the pole and carefully settled it on one side of the boat. He headed back up to the hotel kitchen. They would be taking a pot of beans, which the father himself had prepared, and one of rice. The people here on the coast didn't know how to cook them properly, the father always used to say, so if you wanted to eat a good plate of beans, you had to make it yourself. Picking up the pots, Mario muttered, "Old bastard thinks he's the cow that shits the biggest turds. Any dumb-ass can cook some beans. It's not rocket science."

Resentment warmed his skin, but only frosty gusts reached his heart.

The cluster of bungalows was called Hotel Playamar.

He put each pot in a plastic bag and then placed them both in an empty Styrofoam cooler, no ice, where they nestled snugly together, and carried the cooler out to the boat. *I'd better not forget the arepas*, he thought, and went back to the kitchen. *The old bastard will kill me if I leave those behind.* Along with the bag of arepas and the soft drinks, he grabbed the large, very sharp knife that the cook used to slice the fish into steaks. He stashed the arepas in the cooler with the beans, and the Coca-Colas in one of the coolers with ice that they'd use later for storing the gutted fish. He tucked the knife into the cooler too, since he couldn't think of where else to put it. He'd forget to move it somewhere else, and his father, once they were out at sea, would tell him to open the cooler and hand him his first Coca-Cola:

"What's that for?"

"Just in case."

"In case what?"

You're a total loser, the father was always insinuating whenever he spoke to his sons.

Mario went back to his bungalow to collect the bottle opener and his fishing rods, but first he went by his mother's bungalow to see whether she was sleeping or talking with the throng. Nora had turned off the air conditioner and was sleeping, or at least she wasn't talking, though you could still sense the crowd of people. The throng was always there, whether she was awake or asleep. Mario didn't make any noise. He didn't want to wake her up if she was sleeping, or let her know he was there, since they were going to be leaving soon and she'd try to start talking to him. Mario didn't think *Poor thing* or *What a sad life*. The twins never thought or talked about their mother in those terms;

they'd simply been by her side forever and had done everything they could to make sure she didn't suffer any more than God, who didn't exist, had decided she should. And when some unwitting guest, out of nosiness or empathy, told them her life was too hard, they'd respond, "You think so?" and the tourist would refrain from offering any further opinions after that.

The father, his chest furred with gray hair, his legs muscular and veiny, emerged from the darkness, shirtless and wearing athletic shorts, carrying the cast net over his shoulder and a mesh backpack full of sardines and shrimp to use as bait. He came up to the boat and put the bait in the other cooler with ice. To someone looking in from the outside, who couldn't see the orange glow of hatred in the son's belly nor the greenish flame of contempt in the father's, time would seem to keep flowing the way it always had.

The father saw that everything was ready but didn't say anything. Mario felt relieved, and then angry.

"Where's Javier?" his father asked.

"I'll go get him."

Mario went to his brother's bungalow and, just as he expected, found him in the living room, reading in his hammock under the bulb dangling from the ceiling, wearing yellow athletic shorts and a red nylon waterproof jacket. Javier had the same intense black eyes as the father. He was slightly nearsighted and wore a pair of small, sturdy glasses that always fogged up in the sea spray and he'd clean them with the little towel he kept draped around his neck when they went out in the boat. There were books all over the bungalow: in the living room, in the three bedrooms, and even in the bathroom and kitchen, not in bookcases but piled in stacks of ten to fifteen, as if it were some kind of warehouse or storage facility.

On the floor beside the hammock were his fishing rods, the plastic bucket with the reels, and the woven Arhuaco bag where Javier always carried a book, a pack of cigarettes, a pocketknife, and an assortment of smaller fishing supplies: hooks, sinkers, and so forth. He also carried a jam jar of marijuana and a pipe. When he smoked pot on the boat, Javier tried to keep the smoke from blowing toward his father, who disapproved and always told him to knock off smoking that crap. Beside the bag were the four large thermoses they always took with them, full of very sweet, very strong coffee, and a plastic bag with ten unpeeled hardboiled eggs.

"Are we ready?" Javier asked.

Mario was steering the boat. The father, though he'd grown up in the mountains, considered himself a better boatman than his sons, but for a while now he'd enjoyed lounging as they sailed, the wind on his weathered, handsome, clean-shaven face. He was seventy-one years old and looked sixty. A bolt of lightning sliced through the sky at the horizon, like a crack extending down the side of a bowl. Mario grabbed the Evinrude's steering arm with his left hand. The sea was a black mirror.

5:00 a.m.

Nora had sensed the twin's presence, but she preferred to let him think she was sleeping. The engines squealed like a hog at slaughter, and the chorus of prophets chanted from the ceiling:

"Distant murmurs that illuminate the stars. Squall that trembles and chatters."

"Yes," Nora replied. "These things happen. That's life."

December twenty-ninth. On the twenty-third her husband, the King, had with his own hand stabbed a pig down on the beach that had been making such a racket it sounded like a dozen pigs and the boat is moving away moving away. Dawn won't be long now.

"It keeps dawning and dawning. What for?" Nora wondered aloud.

"Feverish sun that chars the beaches, sun that lays waste," the throng prophesied, though the scorching sun that did the father such harm was still many hours off.

The ceiling of pine planks was low and oppressive, but it was cold in the bungalow. They'd taken Nora's fan away after the night she stuck her fingers into its blades, and she'd suffered the heat for a long time because the father refused to buy her an air conditioner. When the twins bought one with their own money, the father initially refused to install it because of the electricity cost, but in the end he relented and now the whole world shivered when she forgot to turn it off.

"Knock-knock," someone said at the door.

It was Doña Libe, a neighbor who came by every morning with her youngest daughter and invited Nora to take a walk on the beach. Sometimes she went with them and sometimes she didn't.

"Who's there?"

"Orange you glad it's Doña Libe!"

Nora wanted to walk. Doña Libe and her daughter always came before sunrise and the three would watch the slow birth of light on the mangroves. The daughter was sixteen years old and mentally retarded. The neighbor was pale-skinned, not very tall, about fifty years old, stout and thick-waisted. She was always wearing a bathing suit and had her eyes all made up. They saw the first herons emerge from the trees where they'd been sleeping and wing their way toward the swamp that lay to the south. Doña Libe asked if the boys had ended up going out this morning, and the throng was about to start singing, prophesying to the neighbor, just imagine it, the possible disaster awaiting them, when Nora hissed at them and signaled and winked and made other movements with her eyes to keep Doña Libe from noticing:

"Shhh, all of you shut up. Not now! What are you thinking? Idiots!"

"Who are you talking to, Doña Nora?" Doña Libe asked, smiling. She and her husband owned a small hotel half a league away, off in the direction the herons were flying in.

"Me?"

"Yes, Doña Nora."

"Nobody, why?"

"Oh, nothing," the neighbor answered in a singsong voice, smiling again.

Out at sea there was no sign of disaster. The lights of the trawlers were visible further out and, not far from shore, the little lights of the smaller fishing boats headed to the spots where they would drop anchor.

"You see?" Nora told the members of the chorus sternly, scolding them for giving Doña Libe the opportunity to pry.

They'd been walking along with the water up to their ankles.

Doña Libe was illuminating the sea foam with the flashlight. To their left, the crabs scuttled in terror across the pure white sand of the gulf, as if the Final Judgment had been announced and they were looking for holes to crawl into to elude God. To the right the throng was now moving along in silence, but a few of them got in the way and blocked her view, and Nora had to lean sideways a little to see the lights out at sea.

"Move out of the way, would you? You're blocking my view," she told them in a voice that had grown strangely flutelike because of her illness, and the neighbor looked at her curiously. But not the little girl, who because of the confusion in her brain didn't engage much with her surroundings.

That's the direction the boat would go.

Nora thought about her sons and wished for them to return unharmed. The chorus misinterpreted her concern as permission to begin chanting: "Watery moon that glimmers. Moon that crucifies verse."

"Hey now, hey. Everybody pipe down," Nora interrupted in her frail voice.

"They talk a lot, huh?" Doña Libe remarked, always kind and willing to put herself in other people's shoes.

They were blocking Nora's path. Her worry about her sons in the boat was blocking her path too. The throng, in chorus, seemed eager to proclaim it, and she to shush them so her neighbor wouldn't notice. Nora didn't discount the possibility that Doña Libe was part of the plot against her hatched by the death squadrons on her husband's orders, and she eyed her neighbor suspiciously, seemingly ready to believe she was part of a conspiracy.

"He's a bootlicker," she said suddenly, furious as a bird, referring to the president. "A lackey, a lackey!"

"Oh, you shouldn't talk about people like that, Doña Nora," the neighbor said. She didn't know what lackey meant, but it hadn't sounded very nice to her.

They walked past Doña Libe's hotel and waved to her husband, who, in the light of the streetlamps, was watering the lawn with the hose as if it were a phallus, Nora thought to herself. He was dark-haired, tall, with a mustache, sixty or so, and his light eyes gleamed when he smiled. They kept walking toward the marsh, past the vacation houses that belonged to people from Medellín, which were occupied by their owners at this time of year. It was five thirty in the morning, and the owners and caretakers were still asleep. Nora stood looking at the slabs with marine designs set into the wall of one of the houses until Doña Libe gently tugged her by the elbow and managed to get her spirit to relinquish those images of ships and sunsets that had her so engrossed. Then the three of them went back to the part of the beach where the still-dark water soaked their ankles.

"Don Alberto looks like the devil," Nora said suddenly, and the neighbor smiled with pleasure, besotted.

"Devilishly handsome and gallant," she agreed. "Isn't that right, sweetie? Isn't your father very handsome?"

"Yes."

The neighbor said the girl had ended up a little dim after a bout of meningitis, but Nora always thought she'd been ill-constructed from the beginning. It looked like she'd been cut clumsily out of a piece of cardboard with scissors and ended up with a flattened skull, a large hooked nose, and very close-set eyes.

"Simmer down, all of you!" she shouted as a preventive measure. Where a captain rules, a sailor has no sway, she thought. Hopefully the twin would stab the sailor's captain. And hopefully not. He could also drown him – they say it's a sweet death. A sweet death in saltwater, what do you say to that.

Out on the smooth sea, the fishermen's canoes looked like little scratch marks. *They're going to empty out the sea. They aren't going to leave anything for my boys*, Nora thought bitterly.

"Oh dear, I don't know when I'll be able to take a vacation," she said then, a weary expression on her face, and this time the neighbor looked sincerely moved and surprised.

"And where is it that you work, Doña Nora, if you don't mind my asking?"

"The Ministry of Foreign Affairs, with all those nobodies."

They walked almost to the little huts right at the edge of the marsh. Soon they would fill up with tourists who'd come in on buses from Sincelejo and Montería to spend the day dancing, eating, drinking, and swimming in the sea. Now the sand was clean and swept, impeccable, and it seemed impossible that in just a few hours it would all be covered in refuse. One Sunday afternoon, Nora had come with her children and spotted the tidy cylinder of a piece of human excrement bobbing in the sea, rolling on the waves, while the crowd of oblivious tourists, who had arrived early to start strewing paper and bottles everywhere, splashed around beside it. Now, whenever she saw the palm-thatched huts, Nora always felt the urge to turn back. It was as if that cylinder was still there, rolling on the waves, waiting for her.

They returned home, where the neighbor said goodbye and went off with the little girl, who never said goodbye.

"Storm that roils the compass. Sextant that cannot find the horizon."

"Yes, I know, you don't have to keep repeating it. It's annoying. You know what? We should have a party instead."

She made sure the doors and windows were firmly shut, turned down the air conditioner, and they had a party.

6:00 a.m.

Javier eyed his father's invulnerable back as the old man, sitting up in the bow, received the morning full on his face.

His father was skinnier and shorter than Javier, and he was wearing a polo shirt that had started out red but had long since faded.

People always told Javier, who was of average height, that he looked a lot like his father and not much like his brother. Mario was blond and slim, like Nora had been before illness had hunched her over or deformed her body or changed her or whatever it had done.

It made no difference to Javier if he resembled his father.

Their relationship wasn't an easy one, but, unlike Mario, Javier had learned to control his emotions. He always tried to keep a level head to avoid making his mother's and brother's lives too complicated. Like Mario, Javier took drugs: cocaine and occasionally speed, since they relieved some of the monotony of coastal life. But he was generally able to keep things under control. At times, like his brother, he'd shut himself up in his bungalow and wouldn't come out again for several days. But he indulged in these fits of melancholy, isolation, alcohol, drugs, and books only during the low season, when there weren't any tourists around, since Javier, like his father and brother, was first and foremost a businessman, and a good one too, disciplined: he wasn't about to squander the high season holing up with a bunch of books, snorting cocaine, and drinking aguardiente.

Javier didn't believe for a minute that he and Mario were failures like the father always said when he'd been drinking, and sometimes even when he hadn't. It didn't bother him that the old man talked that way, but Mario was more sensitive and tended to get his feelings hurt. Sure, they liked doing drugs, Javier wouldn't deny it, but they could pay for their vices themselves. They didn't need to depend on anybody else. They ran the hotel restaurant like clockwork and had, just the two of them, without seeking the father's counsel, bought a little grocery store up on the paved road that brought in good profits.

He pulled the pack of Pielrojas out of his bag, turned his back to the wind, and lit a cigarette. Mario was looking too quiet and concentrated, so Javier jerked the steering arm. *Lord knows what this dumb-ass is daydreaming about now*, he thought. The Evinrude was practically brand-new and made a steady sound. He liked the way the motorboat leaned back when Mario accelerated. It had been pricey, but expensive things come out cheaper in the long run, Javier thought. They reached the tip of the pincer that closed off the northern end of the gulf and headed toward the first island in the archipelago, near where they were planning to fish.

Out to sea, in the northwest, a mass of gray, almost black clouds had gathered, the distant stone-colored downpour lit by bolts of crisscrossing lightning that swelled and ebbed in intensity but never went out. It was as if in the distance a sort of fire was raging. The rest of the sea, the rest of the universe, was serene and blue.

He poured himself some coffee from a thermos and sipped it as the turquoise water rushed swiftly under the boat. Out at sea, the storm's display intensified. Nobody really felt like talking, especially not about landscapes, so they didn't say much, but now and then one of them would turn his head to look at it.

The island appeared on their right, with its coconut palms and thatched huts and camping tents and the campers' clothing draped on the mangroves' lower branches, and they kept going till it disappeared again and there was only water everywhere you looked.

The father said "here," and they dropped anchor.

They started catching fish as soon as the hooks hit the water. They pulled out mojarras, red snappers, large sea bass, and all of them flopped around, rainbow-colored, in the bottom of the boat. Sometimes they stunned them with a stout cudgel; sometimes they didn't have time to club them because they had to focus on reeling in the other lines. This kind of abundance wasn't an everyday thing. They were catching blue runners, king mackerel, crevalle jacks. Javier had to stop and take a rest. He smoked a cigarette and then rummaged in his bag for the jar of marijuana and lit his pipe, making sure the smoke didn't waft over to his father.

7:00 a.m.
I'm the old tourist in bungalow five. It has the best view of the ocean, even if the toilets are stubborn flushers and the window screens don't do much to keep the mosquitoes out. My eldest granddaughter and her husband brought me here. We old people wake up early, which is why I was up to spot the father through the blinds when he went out with the fishing net and the twin when he lit the Coleman lantern and started getting the boat ready. I went back to bed, not to sleep but to wait for daylight. I heard the motor start up. When you get to my age, the nights seem endless. Even the noise of the waves stretches them out,

and you can't tell anymore if life is lasting for ages or going by in a flash, with seconds that crawl along like slugs and weeks that race over a cliff. But I fell asleep anyway. When I woke up it was daytime and I'd already forgotten about the father and his boys.

We're the tourists.

I'm the seven-year-old girl from Medellín with the pale blond hair who stepped on a catfish and got stung. A little black boy peed on my foot to get the poison out. My parents and two aunts and I got here yesterday when it was almost nighttime. I woke up in the morning and ran outside to jump into the ocean, and wasn't even in up to my knees when, bam, I stepped on the fish and its dorsal spine stabbed me in the foot. I never noticed the hotel owner or his sons, but I remember the awful pain and the warmth of the boy's pee. "Why did you let him pee all over you?" my mother asked when she got down to the beach. "It was just her foot, ma'am," the boy said. She didn't even look at him. We're about to go out and find a doctor.

Or I'm the grandmother, born and raised deep in the mountains of Antioquia, who'd never been to the seashore before and whose shoulders and thighs burned in the sun when nobody was paying attention, and who ended up having to be slathered with milk of magnesia in her bungalow to treat the blisters. With all that going on, I don't know or care what might happen to those men out at sea. What I know is blisters and the feverish deliriums of sun poisoning and the fear of death.

And I'm the drunk tourist who didn't see a thing because he fell asleep on the beach at ten at night, but who knows only too well what it's like to wake up at seven in the morning with the sun beating down, sprawled on the sand with a nearly empty bottle in one hand and a belly full of regret.

Everybody gets hunches, and we tourists are no exception, but, truth be told, they're often wrong. Like maybe I feel like it's going to rain, and half an hour later the sun comes out. When it comes to that stuff, the locals here look at us like we're babes in arms: we may see all the same things they do, but we don't know anything about the sea. Cast a hook and line for me, and watch me get everyone on the boat tangled up in it. So the real fishermen, like the father and the twins, would rather not take us out with them. But we tourists came here to have a good time, so we laugh about that and about lots of other things. We aren't going to be here on the gulf forever: we're bank employees, grade-school or graduate students, toddlers, cab drivers, retirees, housewives. Too bad for the people who are stuck here forever, shackled to these waters, this punishment.

We found out Nora's punishment had started a long while back, when they were living in Montería. The father was never in love with her; he married her only because he didn't want to leave her alone with the boys. He's rarely hit her, and he's always made sure her needs are met, but he's never bothered hiding his numerous affairs, which he carried out right under Nora's nose, and definitely never worried about the psychological trauma they might cause her and the boys.

A little while back he brought a young woman, Iris, to live with him at Playamar. She came with her kid and everything. If you tried to talk to the father about psychological trauma, he'd look at you as if you were speaking Russian, or he might even laugh in your face. Of course, here on the gulf you rarely get a tourist who knows about psychological trauma and triggers and talks about these sort of things. Tourism around these parts is more recreational than it is intellectual – it features way more liquor than it does books, at least during the high season. You don't tend to see bookworms on these beaches; they shrink from the exuberant noise and happiness. A few do come in low season, and when they show up Javier talks to them and listens closely to what they have to say. It's from them that he learned about the psychological triggers of schizophrenia and other topics that his father, if you put him on the spot, would probably judge "a crock of nonsense."

Nothing escapes our notice, not even things that happen when we're not around. We always end up hearing about them from somebody who was there, a local from these parts. Nothing stays hidden from us for long – not even what was or wasn't going to happen in that motorboat out on the water once the island was lost from view and they dropped anchor. Not even what was going to happen afterward, on their way back.

I'm the sociable guy who somehow ended up alone in life at fifty-seven – though I do have a couple of cousins in Remedios – and spend my days walking up and down the beach, chatting with everyone and no one. In Medellín I rent a room from two old ladies near the Plazuela de San Ignacio; they like me a lot, and I like them. I eat breakfast, lunch, and dinner with three other retirees. I used to work at Siemens, and the first thing I tell people I meet here on the coast – and I meet a lot of people, with all my walking and chatting – is that I used to work at Siemens.

And I ask things.

"So the islands are off that direction?"

"That direction, yes sir," the fisherman replies, standing next to his boat. He's black. Laconic. Disdainful. He's not about to tell some tourist that he hasn't gone out fishing today because he's afraid of rough seas.

"There's really good fishing out there, they tell me."

"Good fishing."

"Are they far?"

"A little far," the fisherman says, and then he warms up a bit and decides to give me the information. "About two hours in a good boat. Three hours in mine."

Worn out from having to make such an effort with the conversation, he goes off to have an ice-cold beer in a bar on one of the streets leading to the park, and this time he has better luck with the woman behind the counter. He's the affable lone tourist. He's in the largest town along the gulf shore, Tolú, which some people say is a contraction of Todoluz – full of light – twenty minutes by taxi from the Hotel Playamar, where he's staying. And so the tourist and the woman talk happily about some topic, any topic, it doesn't matter what.

Or I'm the forty-year-old man, father of three little girls with light-colored eyes, ten, nine, and six years old, and the owner of a Toyota SUV that gets a lot of admiring looks here at the beach, from everybody, whether they know anything about cars or not. He's an experienced businessman, this tourist. He's got capital and claims to be looking to buy a few businesses or properties along the seafront. The night before, he and the father sat talking in one of the hotel's pretty little palm-thatched shelters on the beach, eating hunks of fried pork with fried plantain and corn arepas and drinking aguardiente. The father told the experienced businessman he had two good-for-nothing sons.

If it weren't for them, he said, he wouldn't sell – he'd just asked a hundred million pesos for a property worth maybe forty – but he was tired of running the business all by himself, and it was a good business. The father rattled off some profit figures. According to his numbers, he brought in an impressive amount during the high season. The father said sometimes as many as four buses would arrive from Medellín at one time, all packed with tourists, and he didn't have enough space for everybody, so he'd put up to eight people in one room. And since the price per person was the same either way, well, you do the math. Plus the restaurant. Plus drinks.

Humility isn't one of the father's flaws, and as they kept drinking, Hotel Playamar gradually was transformed into a monument to his genius as a businessman.

He talks a lot when he's drinking, the father does, a lot. It drives Mario, who's quiet and often overhears him saying how the sons are a couple of losers, absolutely crazy. By now the guest was drunk too, though you couldn't tell, since he was good at holding his liquor and seemed sincerely impressed. He's a hypocrite, of course, this tourist is. He doesn't know the first thing about sincerity, and he knew full well the property wasn't worth even half what the father was asking. He knew the old man was caught up in delusions of grandeur, common among the entrepreneurial set, and the tourist wasn't criticizing that fervor at all. He took it for granted, considered it par for the course in a good businessman. The tourist didn't have the slightest intention of buying property, even though he had the money, and the father knew full well the other man had no intention of buying anything, even if he could. But the two of them were engaged in a sort of symbiosis: the tourist let the father indulge in delusions of commercial grandeur and lavish praise of the gulf; the tourist, for his part, got to enjoy being treated like someone special, not one of those goobers in terry-cloth shorts who showed up on the buses from Medellín, but a first-class A-plus VIP who'd cruised up with his family in the most gawked-at and coveted SUV around.

Whenever the father talks about the gulf, he waxes poetic and extols the beauty of the sunsets and the color of the sea. For some reason that really pisses Mario off, really makes him want to kill him. The father also talks about how peaceful life is there, though just then music blaring from a passing truck will almost drown out his remark and even the sound of the waves. And he sings the praises of the unsullied environment, though the twin knows full well – and doesn't actually care – what they do with the sewage at the hotel.

When Mario hears his father talking with the tourist, he wishes a lightning bolt would flash down from the night sky and strike the two of them. The guest, for his part, when the father starts in again on what a burden the twins are, muses that a man shouldn't speak ill of his children, especially when they're right there listening, but he doesn't say anything. Everybody's got to raise his kids his own way. He'd rather cut out his own tongue than speak ill of his daughters, whom he adores, just as he adores his wife, and all of them adore him back. *To each his own*, he thinks, not without a certain alcoholic melancholy, as he sees Mario appear in the light of the snack hut to serve a little boy and then head back out into the shadows.

And I'm Yónatan, the boy who bought the small can of condensed milk from the twin at the snack hut that time. I'm seven years old, I'm in first grade at the La Salle school in Envigadò, Antioquia, and when the twin handed me my change, one of the bills was a raggedy thousand-peso note. His father, the hotel owner, was drinking with another man at one of the tables on the beach, and the twin kept looking over at them. I stood there holding the bill in my hand. The twin stopped looking at the men.

"What's wrong?" he asked.

"Can you exchange this bill, please?" I said.

"Exchange it? You a pussy or something? Money's money. It's old, but it's money. Go on, scram. I'm busy," said the twin, who looked over at the men again and left the hut.

I tucked the change into my shorts pocket, trying to keep the thousand pesos from falling apart.

So the young tourist went off with his thousand pesos in his pocket and guzzled down the condensed milk until the sweetness made him cough and scratched the back of his throat.

The next day the father and the twins would go out and experience the great abundance of fish mentioned earlier, and then the absence of fish, and then the run of big tarpon, and the swell, and the pounding of the waves.

8:00 a.m.

They were catching so many, there was no time to club and stun them, so the fish flopped around on the floor of the boat like a frenzied rainbow, their odor strong but by now deeply familiar. *We can't take on more than a thousand pounds anyway, or this thing will sink with the slightest swell*, the father thought. *We'd have to throw the sodas overboard. And the beans. And one of the twins.* He smiled at his joke. There was a violent tug on one of the lines, the reel shrieked, and he started to pull in his catch, which, from the way it was fighting, seemed like it might be a crevalle jack or a really big horse-eye jack.

The storm they'd seen off to the northwest still had solid contours, like slabs of stone, but it had at least tripled in size and was moving toward the coast. The father pulled a beautiful golden crevalle jack, almost three feet long, out of the water and gave it two sharp blows, then looked at the storm, his mind empty. It was still far enough away that they couldn't hear the rumble of the thunder.

"Come on, get to work, idiot," he told Javier, who'd stopped for another smoke. "You should have just stayed home if all you're going to do is sit on your ass."

Javier didn't say anything. He rarely answered back, and maybe that was why his father had fewer problems with him. The other twin was cocky and had earned himself a shout and a slap on more than one occasion. The father doesn't like hitting his sons, but sometimes it's the best way, since it clears the air and everything works out better. Despite Nora's madness and his complicated relationship with his sons, the father thinks, when looked at the right way, and especially given the prosperity the hotel has brought them, things have turned out pretty well.

Everybody's got problems.

The hotel was worth a hundred million pesos; the jeep, ten; the parcel of land across the highway behind the hotel, where he's planning to expand once it becomes necessary, another twenty; and the house in the village, fifty. What else? He's forgetting something. Oh, right, and the house in Medellín, where three of his sisters, the ones who aren't married, live rent-free; it's worth a hundred million or a hundred fifty million. The father was about to start adding it all up when he felt a tug on one of the rods and after a few minutes reeled in a sea bass weighing about a pound, pound and a half.

The world is a horn of plenty.

The night before, he'd sat around until ten with the guest who was talking about buying the hotel, and then he'd gone to bed. The father had an ascetic streak. If he drank, it was only as part of his job catering to tourists, and if he made showy displays of his wealth and his contempt for his sons, it was partly out of vanity but also to make sure his guests had an enjoyable, interesting stay. And of course he never drank too much or let it get in the way of his business. His amiability was shot through with a streak of frigidity and a sort of disdain for tourists, like you might feel for a fool or the goose with the golden eggs, precisely because the fool and the goose allowed themselves to be taken advantage of. There was a tinge of violence in his notion of the hotel industry and related enterprises.

What he found impossible to accept – and the astute tourist could sense this impossibility – was the idea that, even though they were great fishermen, he and the twins were not of the sea. That particular arrogance, the presumption of knowing the sea, has led to disaster for as long as the sea and human history have existed. The boys had practically been born on the gulf, it's true, but they were still landlubbers, not unlike the tourists in some ways. The three of them were expert fishermen, and the father had even won contests for landing the largest swordfish and grouper, but no fisherman descended from a line of gulf fishermen would have stayed out at sea in those conditions. Many of them wouldn't have gone out at all that day. But the greed of the hobbyist, and perhaps an excess of sun, had conspired to cloud the father's judgment, and at some point, after night had already fallen, it would become clear even to him that something might go wrong – and Javier would tell him that, but either the father didn't hear him or he pretended not to.

At eight thirty in the morning, the sun mingled with the turquoise sea, and the boat and the three of them floated in an eternal splendor. They pulled in seven- or eight-pound king mackerel, forty-pound red snapper that would sell for eight thousand pesos a plate. His hotel and the neighboring ones were full, so that meant eighty people – the restaurant's maximum capacity – at eight thousand pesos each. Tourists always ate quickly – they were voracious after staying in the water till their eyes were red with salt and their fingers and toes as wrinkled as raisins – and pretty soon they'd get up from the table to go off for a nap, so the restaurant was able to serve maybe a hundred customers a day at lunch. *Eight thousand pesos a plate. The plantain barely costs anything. Rice costs even less. Two slices of tomato, four shreds of cabbage. You do the math.*

The father didn't consider himself greedy or stingy, just pragmatic. It didn't make sense, for example, to do up the bungalows with lots of luxurious touches when they were going to be booked solid regardless. The guests had come to the beach; they didn't care about the heat. They could make do, and a lot of them drank aguardiente to help them sleep. He gave them fans, of course, and good mosquito nets – they're really expensive, those nets, and they see some hard use – so the guests would be able to sleep without sheets, unmolested by heat or mosquitoes. *No little decorations on the walls or cheesy knickknacks; no shower curtains, since the guests never bother closing them and everything gets wet anyway – they're the ones who have to mop it up, not me. Tourists don't take care of things; why waste gunpowder shooting chickens? If they want five-star hotels, they can go to Cartagena and pay an arm and a leg to swim in the sea there, which is full of mercury, not clean like the waters of this beautiful gulf.*

He kept baiting the hooks and hauling them back in loaded with fish, their many servings of flesh already sold and eaten before they left the water. Forty or fifty pelicans flew over the boat in a V, accompanied, as always, by silence. Though he was annoyed when Javier stopped to look at them, this time he didn't say anything and instead felt an involuntary thump of compassion for his two children, as if from up there in the sky he'd suddenly been shat on by a seagull.

The poor kids had wound up with a real headcase for a mother.

People love running their mouths, but none of it was my fault, he thinks as he reels in a line that's been robbed of its bait. *Everybody's responsible for his own life. She was already a little screwy when we got married, and maybe that's why she quickly forgot what I'd told her: I was doing it for the kid, but I wasn't made to be faithful to any woman. She'd have her house, her food, her nice clothes, and she and the kid – who turned out to be two kids – would never want for anything. But I was born to be free. When I married her, I'd already seen a fair bit of life. I left home when I was practically still a boy. I was selling pots and pans door to door in the villages before I'd turned fifteen, not like these two good-for-nothings – they don't have a clue what it means to have to hustle to make a living. Sometimes they seem like spoiled brats.*

Mario had caught almost as many fish as his father. *He's a good fisherman, you've got to give him that, unlike his brother, who spends hours in a stoned haze. He's good at pulling them out of the water once they're hooked, Javier is, but not so good at hooking them.* No matter what the father says or thinks, there's some element in his relationship with Javier that he has a hard time acknowledging. Though he almost never says anything positive about the young man, he can't help respecting him. It may be that the books have something to do with that respect, since, though the father has read very few, he's well aware a person can't go around making fun of Shakespeare, for example, and saying he was a loser or a flaming queer. The father is an intelligent man. He knows that no individual, not even him, understands everything about the world, and so he recognizes that human beings will be forever doomed to humility. He's seen the way Javier remains unflappable despite his crazy mother and how he's preserved his optimism and good sense over the years. With some degree of pride, he concludes that Javier's strength and maturity are due in large part to the father himself, who has always been a model of steadfastness and intransigence.

But the twins do sometimes go off and take drugs, and that shiftlessness has been an endless source of scorn and worry for him. When that happens, he confronts the boys and rants loudly and at length about what a burden they've been, how weak they are, how much they owe him. "Let's be frank here. Look how you shut yourselves up in your rooms to rot away – you don't even eat. You're going to end up like your mother, I'm telling you." The cook and the other employees overhear him, as do the guests, the former admiringly, the latter faintly shocked.

Stretching before them, always, is the water, sometimes gray-green, sometimes turquoise blue. The air is filled with herons and gannets moving against the blue sky. In summer, like now, the heat is powerful, dry, gusty. During the rainy season, when the boys tend to go off and smoke and do drugs, the humidity and heat are intense and melancholy, and the storms are massive and threaded with lightning.

The father hooks a barracuda that dashes from one end of the boat to the other. He has to shove his sons out of his way, and in the scuffle they nearly capsize and lose the two hundred pounds of fish they've already caught. The line suddenly goes slack as it snaps, and the father's elation evaporates in an instant, his euphoria replaced with fury directed at the twins, who have gotten in his way, at the sea, at the fish. He shivers a little with the cold.

He's well aware his sons would be pleased to see him defeated.

9:00 a.m.

He'll haul on that line till it snaps on him, the old bastard, thinks Mario, who has not overtly hindered his father, though he did exhibit a certain lethargy while his father was battling with the fish.

He watches the father sit down on the second bench, defeated, take out two hard-boiled eggs and an arepa, crack the eggs against the gunwale of the boat with unnecessary force, peel them disdainfully, drop the shells on the cushion of fish splashing in the bottom, salt the eggs, and begin to eat, gazing out at the water with his intense black eyes. Mario decides to wait for his father to finish eating and return to his own bench so he can get his breakfast without having to go near the old man.

"Pass me a thermos," the father says, and Mario pretends not to hear him. "Pass me the thermos, will you, don't play dumb with me," he says, and Mario, leaning against Javier's shoulder as his brother reels in one of the lines, picks up the thermos but doesn't hand it to him, instead placing it on the bench between his father's bench and Javier's, where his father will have to get up in order to reach it.

The air is less chilly now, and you can feel the mallet of the sun descending.

When the father, holding his coffee, moves back toward the prow and away from the food cooler, Mario leans again against Javier's shoulder – his brother has just pulled the hook out of a little shark less than two feet long and is about to toss the animal back into the sea – and takes out two eggs and two arepas. But his father is still relatively close by, so Mario's movements are unconsciously too quick and somewhat furtive, like those of a thieving monkey. *Old bastard*, he thinks when he realizes that, in his hurry, he's forgotten the salt. He asks Javier to pass it to him, and his brother stops baiting his hook and tosses the salt-shaker so Mario can catch it in the air. Mario has been calling his father an "old bastard" since early adolescence.

"Who're you calling dumb, you old bastard?" he mutters now between clenched teeth.

"What's that? What did you say? Speak up when you talk, would you? That way we'll be sure to understand each other."

"Hey, hey, cut it out, you two. Shut up and let me fish."

During the period that had followed his awakening to consciousness – in those days of euphoria at the presence of the sun, the sea, the world – Mario had even felt great affection for his father. Those were the days when his father and the sea and the mangroves were one and the same. His father and the canoes and the boats and the outboard motors. His father and the cast nets and the hooks and the rods. Nobody could have imagined back then that the boy's fondness would begin to fade rapidly before adolescence and end up transformed into resentment.

The boy had spent those fishing trips with his father in wonderment as they moved through the mangrove swamp, full of silence and noise, darkness and light. He was eight or nine years old. *With dripping oars suspended above the water, we floated silently through the mangroves, our lives stilled amid the hubbub of nearby birds*, the twin would have reminisced, had he been the sort of person given to words. *The morning light descended from the sky and grew heavy as it fell through the branches and plunged into the water, seeking the origin of the mangroves as they rose out of the mud and caressed the water with their branches.*

With the flashlight, the father would show the twins those stretches of water in the mangrove swamp where, at a little before six in the morning, the night remained intact. In them, the caimans' eyes gleamed. *High in the mangroves, the herons glowed as if they contained the origin of light. And in the dense water, farther off, were the caimans. In the bottom of the canoe, all tied together, six crabs waved their legs and pincers, and I'd also caught a few sea bass.*

Around the time when the boy reached the age of reason, the mother began to lose hers. His mother's illness and the twin's suffering in the face of it were equally vast, both full of sound and fury, and for him they were as mute and inexpressible as the magic of the mangrove swamp. Words would never be Mario's strong suit; even as a boy he'd tended toward silence or monosyllables or short sentences. Nor had he ever taken pleasure in books or learning. Fishing, the boat, and his love for his mother were all that mattered to him.

Whenever they returned from the sea or the mangrove swamp, the boy would be immersed in his mother's reality, moving from one extreme to another, in a world of pure delusion: the singing of her throng, who would just come to visit at first and eventually stayed for good, and whom he sometimes could even hear; the people who went in and out of the two bedrooms, in the living room and kitchen, on the roof and in the bathroom, and whom he sometimes could even see; and especially the things she said – *Once the baby's born, I'm getting out of this house* – which confused and frightened Mario so much that Javier, to soothe him, would tell him not to pay any attention to her, there was no baby and she wasn't going anywhere. "Don't believe everything she says, you know – she's crazy." Javier was eight or nine, but seemed like he was twelve.

So Mario would get to his mother's house and enter a world of overabundance and fear, a world where the incomprehensible sentences were more compelling than the comprehensible ones, though some of them engulfed the boy from all sides and left him shipwrecked.

"Belladonna flower that grows beside my face," said the mother.

"What?"

"Inerrant night, night of ravens, precious apricot of mine. Right, Mario?"

"Is that a song?"

His mother had gone to college, used strange words, and gave Javier books or read them with him. As long as Mario could remember, his mother's books were always there on the shelves, organized by size, not scattered across the floor like his brother's. Years later she would start burning them one by one in the courtyard, over the course of days, months, cackling to herself very quietly, *teeheeheehee*, like a witch in a movie, until only the empty shelves remained.

"Bird, black bird praying outside my door."

"What?"

The mother would look at him and keep speaking in words suffused with color and a terrible logic that left him frozen there, as if caught in a powerful spotlight. Suddenly tired, the boy would walk toward the door, saying *I'll be back, mamá, I won't be long*. He'd go wander along the beach, and after a while Javier and the manager's boys would show up and they'd all leap into the sea and play in the water with the wooden rollers that the fishermen used to pull the boats up on the beach. They were the motor and the rollers were the boats.

After breakfast, Mario poured himself some coffee too and then passed the thermos to his brother, who was staring off at a spot on the horizon as he ate. The father started baiting the lines, and soon the twins joined in, and once again they started pulling in large king mackerel, crevalle jacks, and nine- or ten-pound snappers, and the pounds kept adding up in the bottom of the boat.

The storm was still far away and hadn't gotten any larger, but it had intensified. There was so much lightning, one on top of the other, that now in the boat they heard a constant rumble, as if somewhere in the distance stones were tumbling over one another. Mario caught a huge sawfish that glinted in the air with metallic flashes after a long struggle in which the nylon fishing line sliced the surface of the water like a knife. The father was grudgingly impressed by the animal, though he didn't say anything and certainly didn't look at the twin. They had more than three hundred pounds now, and they hadn't had time to clean the fish and put them in the coolers, and they were losing hardly any of their catch. The sea was still calm. The father hooked another king mackerel, and fought with it, and pulled it out of the water, and it glistened in the air, larger than the one Mario had caught. A gust of wind blew for a few seconds, as if impelled by a distant blast, and the air went quiet again.

The two king mackerel opened and closed their mouths as they gazed up at the cloudless sky, and sometimes they flopped around there on top of the other fish in the bottom of the boat.

10:00 a.m.

Nora was worn out after the party. Catalina, her lifelong enemy, and the friends of a woman named Carlota had behaved quite abominably, doing things that went far beyond eroticism to filth. Filthy women. And they spent a long time talking about her, in Bulgarian, and laughing with vulgar cackles. Her persecutors were insulting her on her right and her protectors were soothing her on her left. Pleasant in one ear, belligerent in the other. Finally Armando and his chorus arrived and she had relations with all of them.

"I curse the day I failed to reach him," said Nora, who had sat down on the porch to meditate. "Life of pleasures by my side, and here alone without you I am starting over again."

The sun was beating down now. Some brown boobies were plunging like furled umbrellas into the water that would at that moment be surrounding her sons and her husband and, like them, were fishing for fish that looked like stones. Nora rocked back and forth in a chair that wasn't a rocking chair and twisted her hair with one finger until her head hurt and tears nearly came to her eyes. Then she stroked her face with her fingertips. A black dog scuttled by on the ground like a cockroach on the ceiling.

"Boat, boat," said the dog.

"Dungeon he gave her as a pillow," the throng suddenly sang from the coconut palms, startling her. "Far from her life. Far from her home. Perfect image that she would lose. A mischievous life, hers was, playful ever since childhood. Why, when she'd been dreaming tangerine dreams, did her spirit grow ill and her soul shatter into pieces and die, alone, in her hands?"

The echo of the voices reached the mangroves and then the highway and the cattle ranches, farther back, where the zebus were grazing in the still-cool morning. Later they would seek to evade the searing sun in the shadow of the trees.

"Yes," said Nora. "Cursed. May the water take you and carry you away."

On the sand's far horizon, a mirage was forming that became an apparition, then a person, and then a stout woman walking toward her with a wide basket of coconut candy on her head.

"Rhythmically the African population walks to the pounding of drums," the throng intoned.

"Good morning, Doña Nora. I've got your papaya candy, your coconut sweets, your tamarind treats."

"Your tamarind treats!" sang the chorus from the coconut palms.

Nora went to the bungalow's kitchenette to fetch a soup bowl, and the woman filled it with candies that the twins would pay for later. She put a piece of candied papaya in her mouth; it was still warm, and the crunchy sugar flooded her ears with flavor, and she closed her eyes as the delicious sunny sweetness descended and ran all through her.

It didn't matter whether the chorus suspected or did not suspect what was happening at that moment, but they must have known something, Nora thought, since everybody had started to sing:

"Fish, one after another, one, two, three, say thirty-three!"

"See you later, Doña Nora."

"Wind," Nora nodded.

The cockroach skittered past on the sand and the patches of scraggly grass in front of the house. She felt out of sorts, then sad, and said:

"Sea squalls that batter my life."

She knew that high up in the sky, where she couldn't see them, three black gulls were flying, with red beaks and feet, the kind that never fly low and are very beautiful even though they also resemble carrion birds. Swallow-tailed kites. Had the King died? Terrifying, terrifying. Had Doña Libe come by today? Was the morning already over, the morning of this day on which the imponderable was bearing down on the sea? Nora's time, like everybody else's, always moved in just one direction, toward the origin, but it was raked by powerful, disorienting winds.

She ate the whole plate of papaya and coconut candies and then craved salt. She'd had an early breakfast – eggs and boiled cornmeal dumplings – and now she wanted bread with costeño cheese and a cold glass of Colombiana soda. Nora ate too much and had gotten fat. The beautiful figure she'd had before the madness was long gone. "I had gorgeous legs – everybody wanted to eat me up," she would say from time to time, out of the blue, making people uncomfortable. The medications damaged her teeth, and now she was missing several incisors. She rarely brushed her hair, though she enjoyed taking baths, and she spent much of the day in a robe or slip.

Wearing a slip, Nora went to the hotel kitchen and asked the cook for bread and costeño cheese and sat down in a chair to eat. The sea wasn't visible from there, but you could hear it. In the mornings the waves rolled slowly in the gulf and got rougher as the day went on. The salty costeño cheese had to be eaten in small bites and with lots of bread. The local bread was almost sweet; the Colombiana, very cold, spicy from all the carbonation, foamy. Suddenly the chorus started chanting so loudly that Nora couldn't hear what the cook was saying to her, much less what the sea was murmuring a hundred meters away:

"Rarefied sun. Vengeance. Gale, stone, and wall."

"Yes," Nora answered heatedly, unable to hear what the cook was still saying. "Cancellation and stupor."

The cook finished saying what she'd been saying, whatever it was, smiled, and floated off, round as a balloon, to work at the counter beside the stove. The chicken flew up, split into pieces, and plunged into the stewpot. With two strokes of the knife, the plantain lost its tips and was flayed. Another three rapid strokes chopped it into pieces and it, too, dropped into the abyss. A little cloud of cumin floated in the air. Then a larger cloud of annatto, as if a sapote-colored demon had opened its wings above the pot of what would become sancocho stew. Ten filets of sea bass were waiting, pellucid, on a cutting board. The manioc was white, like the nape of an angel's neck. Horrible! The tropics, the tropics, thought Nora.

Wind.

Javier pulled out the pipe and marijuana again and took a drag, holding back the smoke, silently releasing it and making sure it didn't blow toward his father. The calm that sometimes emanated from things was something the old man had never managed to enjoy and could not understand. It was fine to like money and business dealings – greed makes the world go 'round, thought Javier – but there was no need to get irritated about everything else.

The sun beat down on the boat from the cloudless sky.

Javier pulled three mandarin oranges out of his bag and tossed one to Mario and another to his father. They caught them without thanking him and peeled the fruit, and a mandarin-scented stain spread over the boat, the intense flavor invading them all, especially – since he'd been smoking – Javier. Time passed. They didn't talk much. Javier pondered aimlessly, sometimes thinking, sometimes silently admiring the sea and the sun and how clean they were, sometimes admiring the storm that off to the north had already overpowered the coastline and blotted it out. He thought about Mario. He thought about his father, hatless as the sun grew fiercer by the minute.

He pulled out his clip-on sunglasses and attached them with a click to protect himself from the sun that, despite the bill of his cap, was now making him squint. A blue runner hooked itself on his first fishing rod, and he pulled it out of the water after a struggle that was intense, efficient, brief. The fish kept nibbling. When he ran out of bait, Javier tossed his bowl made of coconut shell so it landed by his father's feet, next to the cooler that contained the backpack filled with sardines and shrimp.

"Some bait, would you?" he said.

In the boat's forty square feet, everything seemed larger and more complicated.

"So the ducks are shooting at the hunters now," the father said.

The bowl had fallen too forcefully into the muddle of water and fish in the bottom of the boat, splashing and humiliating the father. Javier realized that his request for bait had also sounded peremptory, and that all it took was the merest hint of an insult on his sons' part to raise the father's hackles.

"Hunters?" he said, aware that his father knew that he, Javier, had understood and was now playing dumb just to annoy him.

Javier agilely dodged the hurled bowl, which could have given him a deep gash in the bridge of his nose and knocked his glasses off. The bowl landed five meters from the boat, and Mario, without saying anything, dove into the sea and brought it back in two strokes of his arms. Mario climbed out of the water, passed his own coconut-shell bowl full of bait to Javier, and, dripping, headed to the cooler and filled the one he'd just retrieved, careful not to look at the father or bump against him.

Almost noon. The fish were biting less now. Javier thought that if they went back now, they would have had a good day's work anyway, but neither Mario nor his father was going to agree. He estimated they had about four hundred pounds of fish. Most of them were still opening and closing their mouths, and some of them were still flopping around, but as long as more were still biting, he, Mario, and their father would keep fishing – they'd keep going even if the fish stopped biting altogether. There was still the rest of the day and then the night, for deep-water fishing, where you could catch grouper, tarpon, and other large species. Afterward, if the sea got rough, they'd toss the excess overboard.

After the bait incident, the atmosphere became even more tense and the boat seemed to grow heavier. Javier used a coconut-shell bowl to scoop out the water in the bottom of the boat, which now covered the tangled cushion of shuddering or suffocated fish. His movements were precise, swift, those of a person who'd been bailing out boats since he was a kid.

The father, Mario, Javier, the fish, the boat, and the sea itself were a horn of plenty on the brink of the abyss. The breeze was gentle. Things might shift from that serene blue in a fraction of a second, thought Javier, at *any* fraction of a second, to a world of confusion and death.

He finished bailing, stood up, and urinated into the ocean. He thought, *What if I turn around and piss on the old fucker*, but he didn't do it, more out of habitual respect than out of fear. Looking off at the horizon, which was empty of sails and clouds, and without urinating on his father, he stuffed his member back into his shorts and sat down to fish. He was looking after three lines, and he hadn't gotten many breaks so far. He preferred shrimp to sardines, but his father never let him choose his bait when he retrieved it from the cooler.

Between eleven fifty in the morning and twelve noon, nothing happened. Javier's watch was large, the scuba-diving kind, and it glittered on his strong, hairy arm. None of the three caught any fish during that brief period. But there was no need for anything remarkable to happen for existence itself to be remarkable, even admirable, at least for Javier, to whom marijuana presented a world of vast detail and slowness.

From his spot in the boat, he could see his father's hairy arms, very similar to his own. He traced their veins, which looked as if they were carved in wood, and pictured the powerful tree of blood rhythmically swelling his father with the beating of his heart. *His heart must be the size of a green coconut, same as his balls,* Javier thought absurdly. Then he saw a flock of boobies fly overhead, heading toward the coast, and followed them with his gaze and there was the storm. The gray blotch was expanding, more mineral in appearance, lit by lightning in its core as if what was being produced was not sorcery – which is human evil, small-minded evil – but something larger and more impersonal. Through his dark glasses, Javier was also able to surreptitiously observe his brother's profile; Mario's thoughts seemed to be elsewhere as he focused on a bunch of fishing lines, some with cane rods, others wooden, which he cast and then propped one by one carefully along the boat's gunwale. He was also holding a line in his mouth. Mario had already separated out some fish to use as live bait, and they were in a bucket of water, their fins and gills hardly moving, waiting for nighttime, when they would hang on metal hooks, and then grouper and crevalle jacks, in attempting to devour them, would also die. Javier suddenly thought about his father's death. Death's the only thing that exists, he thought, a little overwhelmed by these most recent images the marijuana was bringing him.

As a distraction from his dark thoughts rather than out of thirst, he asked his brother for a bottle of water. His Adam's apple, just below the edge of his perpetual five-o'clock shadow, rose and fell many times as his father watched, seeming to have guessed, Javier thought, what had been passing through his mind.

Noon. He felt his father's gaze on the nape of his neck for a good while. He turned his head when he was sure the old man had stopped looking at him just in time to see the father leap onto one of his rods and almost tumble into the water from the momentum and the fish's pull. The size of the animal that finally emerged from the sea, after a tough fight in which the father seemed to be hauling a motorcycle or a jeep transmission out of the deeps, was startlingly small – only twelve pounds, Javier guessed – in proportion to the tenacious resistance it had exhibited. *That's jacks for you*, he thought. He eyed his father with a certain curiosity; the father looked tense, wound up, triumphant. *The old bastard and the sea*, thought Javier, and he started rummaging for his marijuana pipe in the bottom of his bag.

12:00 p.m.

I'm the tourist taking cover from the blazing noonday sun in his camping tent, sometimes reading and sometimes staring at the sea. I was sitting in a canvas chair on the tent's sort of front patio, under a wide awning made of lime-green nylon held up by two aluminum tubes, light as feathers and strong as bones. My wife and son were sleeping in the tent behind me, her in her bikini and him naked. My son was two years old, very handsome and sturdy and healthy. The tent was excellent, easy to set up, easy to carry – a gift from my wife's sister, who lives in Miami and always buys the most expensive and modern versions of everything. "It's nicer than a lot of the hotels I've stayed in," I told her by way of thanks. In fact, I'd argue it was the best tent on the whole island, the lightest and most waterproof, the most lime-colored, probably the best one that's ever been pitched along these beaches.

I was thirty years old, the same as my wife. Sometimes my desire for her was insatiable and consumed my days. She desired me too, so sometimes love was what consumed our days. The sea is so beautiful at midday. The father and the twins had sailed past that beach a few hours earlier, while we were sleeping. The people on the island knew them, of course, and later commented that it had been quite foolish of them to go out despite the brewing storm.

I'd met the boys a year earlier in Bogotá in the restaurant and bar owned by a mutual friend. They'd been visiting their paternal grandmother, who lived in the Teusaquillo neighborhood. At the bar, the twins told me about their lives. They didn't say much about their mother, except that she was sick, and they didn't speak too harshly of their father. They spoke glowingly of the sea and the mangroves and told me how much I'd enjoy a few days in the hotel, "since you like painting water so much." I had just paid out of my own pocket – or, rather, my pocket, my wife's, and also those of a few friends – to publish an illustrated book of very short poems about the sea, rain, and rivers, a book I handed out in person, one at a time, since in my view that's how poetry should be distributed. I gave a copy to each twin, of course, with a hug and everything, signed.

I liked them, each in his own way. Mario was good-looking, resembling – if you stretched things a bit – one of those young men painted by Renaissance artists. His skin was too tanned and a little blotchy, and his blond curls looked scorched and straw-like from the sun. In his light-colored eyes there was always a glint, a splinter of alarm or terror or anguish, as if a significant part of his soul had been crouched and huddled somewhere since childhood. The two brothers didn't look anything alike. Javier had strong features, like his father's, and just as there was a glint of terror in Mario's eyes, in Javier's there was another, not so much of cruelty or mercilessness, but of audacity, toughness, willingness to push limits. When he started drinking, you began to feel a bit uneasy, since the kind of happiness he exuded was dangerous in the right circumstances. And the circumstances were right that night at our friend's bar. It had gotten late and they were closing up, and I'd been drunk for a while and was crashed out in a chair when Javier got swept up in a brawl and Mario joined in, right outside in front of the place. I heard that ultimately the two of them had made the other guys – I don't know if they were gang members or muggers, but in any event there were a lot of them – drop their knives and run.

Before coming to the coast, I'd gone by one of those wonderful large secondhand bookstores in Bogotá and bought the fifty thousand pesos' worth of books Javier had asked me for. I brought a list of what he already had and chose more according to my own taste. I bought a lot of things he hadn't read or didn't own, but not as many as I'd thought I'd be able to get with that money. Money never goes far when you're buying books, even used ones, and everything ended up fitting into two small cardboard boxes that didn't weigh much. Javier collected the boxes from me at the Montería airport, where he'd come in his father's jeep to pick us up.

Back at the hotel, I didn't get much of a chance to talk with them since they were busy taking care of the other guests. I had a few drinks with Javier the day I arrived and we chatted a little about books and poetry. I didn't see him much after that since he was off taking guests to the swamp in the motorboat or taking them waterskiing. My wife, the baby, and I stayed at Playamar for just three days. There was too much going on – too much noise, too much blaring music by Rodolfo Aicardi and Los Graduados, too many people walking along the beaches clutching bottles of aguardiente – so we decided to go out to the islands.

The woman who sold us lunch after we arrived suggested to my wife that we sleep in her house that night since the tide was high and the water might flood the beach where our tent was pitched and drag us all out to sea. She had a room with three hammocks, so that night we slept in hammocks. Our son made friends with the woman's kids, and it was wonderful to watch him playing with those beautiful black children.

I painted several watercolors of the storm. It was still far away but everybody was saying it might come down on us at any moment: the turquoise blotted out by the gray, by the many grays, which in my watercolors were often dark blues. When I wasn't reading, I painted; when I wasn't painting, I read some very funny novels by someone by the last name of Ibargüen-goitia, the writer with the longest and most complicated last name I've ever read in my life. No matter what I was doing, I was on high alert to whether my wife had taken off or put on her bathing suit, or maybe put on one of those shirts she had, embroidered white cotton, that you could see her breasts through, since she didn't need a bra yet, even after having a child.

"It's like you're made of brown coral," I told her, and she laughed.

"You'd starve if you tried to make it as a romantic poet. Brown coral!" she said, taken aback by the ugly image.

Where did he get such a bizarre image! I was and am his wife, the brown-coral woman, and the mother of our child, who's currently finishing high school here in New York, where we've been living for the past few years. My husband has a hard time – he's convinced I don't really let him get close to me, and he has no idea how much I love him and how close he actually gets. But he can be a little annoying with that high sex drive he's got sometimes. Anyway. I liked the sons and even the father: the father because he was handsome and attentive and helpful and gallant with pretty women like me, and the sons because they were boys, boys, just boys, and they were so touchingly powerless.

While we were at Playamar, I'd gone to the mother's bungalow and we'd talked for a while. She must have been very pretty once, that was obvious, but her teeth were damaged and her face bloated. And she was always saying such funny things.

"Oh, no, sweetheart!" she'd say. "This here is wonderful and all, but Carlota's girls just bobble it up." I asked her who Carlota was and she gestured for me to lean closer so she could tell me in my ear, warily eyeing the planks on the ceiling, which was suffocatingly low, as if Carlota were up there and could hear her. "See that pack of brazen nanny goats? She's their leader," she whispered harshly in my ear, and pointed to the bungalow windows, as if all the nanny goats in Carlota's group were peeping in through the shutters.

They call everything "bungalows" there. A grimy little room was a bungalow and a mafioso's mansion was too, even if it had sterling silver faucets, as long as it was by the beach and had a few things built out of wood. We saw some real dumps where they crammed entire families that came down from the poorer neighborhoods of Medellín. At night those people would roast in the heat because the fans didn't always work. They didn't have much money, poor things, so they just accepted whatever beach lodging they got. David and I went into one of those bungalows out of curiosity, and it turned out to be two rows of rooms, each with a tiny kitchenette and a bathroom so small that the water from the shower fell practically in the toilet. Ten "bungalows" in total, all in a row, under a single roof, across from another row of ten, under another roof, and a patio with a laundry sink in the middle where the tourists washed their underwear and hung it up to dry. The bungalows were all full, so depressing, like a slum, and the clamor was incredible.

Of course they all seemed happy. There were at least two radios blasting. Some kids were running around naked from the waist down, others from the waist up. And in the patio there was also a gorgeous green parrot with a large yellow head. It would whistle the melody to "Los Guaduales," and David said it was the only version of "Los Guaduales" he'd ever enjoyed. Sometimes that dope can be pretty funny. Or at least he seems funny to me.

One afternoon the boys' mother invited me to take a walk along the beach. Her name was Norma, and she was fat and paunchy because her psychiatric medications had boosted her appetite. Not Norma, Nora, Nora. The robe she wore to go out walking came up a little in front, as if she were pregnant. Before we left I felt sorry for her and tidied her hair with a brush I was carrying in my bag so she wouldn't look so disheveled. I put a little of my makeup on her. She smiled at me and I saw she had several teeth missing. And it was strange, really, since her looks were so faded, but you could still tell how beautiful she'd been. Or maybe I just liked her, poor thing, loony as she was.

She talked a lot about how much she loved her boys, both of them, saying they traveled to Egypt and India every week to bring her gifts. "Last week Mario brought me a beautiful sari, just beautiful, from Bombay," she said, and her eyes shone with love for her son. I imagined her all toothless and bloated, swathed in an orange sari.

After that she told me she was a Persian queen. As we walked, I hardly had time to look at the seashells on the beach or the herons flying overhead what with listening to the details of her Persian kingdom, and she didn't stop telling me all about it since she'd come to trust me. We reached a mangrove swamp known as La Caimanera and then turned back. We got to see a gorgeous sunset, with the orange sun sinking into the sea. We stopped to watch. Nora stood in silence and I could tell she felt happy. I hugged her, and we started to cry.

1:00 p.m.

The sun was helping to cloud the father's judgment. He never wore hats because they got in the way, and he was convinced that since he had coarse, curly hair, and a lot of it for his age, growing tight against his skull, the sun couldn't get to him. He was hungover from the aguardiente the night before, and he asked for a beer from Mario, who said all they'd brought was water and Coca-Cola. When the father called him a loser, Mario fired back with an insult, and if the father hadn't been drained by hangover and sun exposure, he would have slapped the twin and a scuffle would have broken out.

The father decreed that they would go buy some beer on one of the islands. He knew the twins weren't happy about making the trip or having their fishing interrupted, and he could even feel it in the air, how much they loathed him. *Where a captain rules, a sailor has no sway. I can't let the boys get the best of me. That's how they'll learn. They can go ahead and hate me if they want*, he thought. *And let's see them try something, if they're so tough.*

They started up the Evinrude and headed for the island. *I can't always be the one taking care of everything*, the father thought. *In this sun, Coca-Cola tastes like cough syrup. Bringing beer instead is just common sense. They've got to learn from their mistakes.*

As the father's bad mood dissipates, he not only starts thinking with fewer curse words but also uses expressions such as "learning from one's mistakes" or "just common sense" – the same ones, in fact, that he always uses when talking to the hotel guests. At one time he'd been in the habit of using them in a conciliatory tone with his sons as well – "It's just fucking common sense to bring some beer along on this kind of trip, Mario, or am I wrong?" he'd have said in this case – but their anger at him had grown and they rejected him by scowling or muttering, convinced he was buttering them up just so they'd forgive him, and his rage would come roaring back all the more powerful and he had to restrain himself from getting violent again.

Back when I was going from village to village on that little Suzuki selling cookpots, I was younger than you two studs, and if I didn't manage to sell all my merchandise or I forgot something, I was the only one who suffered for it. Nobody had to remind me what I needed to do. There goes a school of halfbeak! the father thought in amazement as he watched the long green fish swim past the sky-blue hull in the deep blue-green of the water.

He let his mind wander through the coastal villages, sometimes pretty and sometimes not so much, all of them with beautiful names – San Onofre, Santiago de Tolú, San Bernardo del Viento – that he'd visited with his cookpots back when he was just twenty. There, he'd broken the hearts of more than one young woman and of others who weren't so young anymore. The father was proud of his history with women. "My rap sheet," he called it, using a term coined not by him but a friend of his from Barranquilla, a lawyer, who had a sense of humor that the father could never really match.

And these two don't even have girlfriends. They're still clinging to the skirts of that crazy mother of theirs like little kids. Sometimes I feel sorry for them, especially Mario, who's so . . . Anyway. I'm going to make something of these two morons. They must have inherited at least a little bit of my fire. What they definitely did get, especially Javier – though Mario isn't so bad himself – is a knack for making money. They make things out of nothing, like I did, and they know how to hustle, I've got to admit. Mario does a good job running the restaurant and doesn't let himself get jerked around by the cook or other employees, or the tourists either, even though they can be a real pain in the ass and you have to be firm with them, firm but still letting them feel like they're in charge. Good service is key, but if you're not careful you end up being slave to the first son of a bitch who comes along who's managed to earn himself a couple of pesos and let it go to his head. Like those two French couples who came and were complaining about everything and finally I had to tell them, no, this isn't a five-star establishment, but it's clean and it's got the best beach in Latin America. If you like that, great, I told them, and if not, you know, sirs and madams, nobody's forcing you to be here. And the best part is they stayed, because at the end of the day it's a good hotel, and it's safe, pretty, and cheap.

And the boys' shop has really taken off. They've probably even got money saved up at this point, the clever devils. If they weren't so into their dope, they'd have a car and everything by now, but it's no use beating them or berating them – if they want to go around in a stupor *from marijuana or whatever else they're into, there's nothing I can do about it. I'm just waiting for them to pull themselves together and realize I only push them so hard and get after them for their own good.*

Anyway, the fish have stopped biting so much, so we aren't missing out by going to get beer now. Tonight we'll make up for it with grouper and some big snapper. Look at how pissed they are, especially Mario. His mother has called him "Marito" since he was a little boy, and she spoiled him so much it's a miracle he didn't turn out queer. He's not queer – he likes women, but they don't last. Well, when I was his age they didn't last me all that long either, since I was traveling all over to make a living. Later, when I set up the hardware store in Montería, I didn't move around as much and my girlfriends lasted longer. The problem with Mario is that he kind of gets drunk and mistreats them. And not just verbally. That beautiful girl he was seeing in Tolú, the dark-haired one with the light-colored eyes, the fisherman's daughter – he actually punched her a couple of times in a drunken rage. Her brothers came to me demanding money or else they'd beat the crap out of him, and I told them touch a hair on his head and you'll see what happens, assholes, and didn't give them shit. They didn't do anything. People here on the coast are big talkers but it rarely comes to anything. They told me they were going to dynamite the hotel – that's what they use for fishing sometimes – and I told them go on then, blow it up, you bastards, and I'll come after all of you one after the other. I won't even spare your dogs. After that I went to talk to the girl myself, her with her eyes still all swelled up, and I gave her a little money. The brothers would have taken the money and pissed it away on booze.

Myself, I don't like hitting women. The less, the better, same as with kids. There's almost always a way to straighten things out with an insult or a little shake, and in the long run everybody comes out ahead. It's just common sense. Now this idiot's smoking pot again. It smells like scorched feathers or burning tires, right? I don't know what he sees in that crap.

They're cute when they're little, but eventually they're nothing but trouble. Take Manny, for instance. It's going to be a real shame when he enters that rebellious phase, the way all of them do, and I'll be forced to get tough with him to make sure he grows up straight and doesn't take after these two. I'm going to start him out on the right foot. He's ahead of the game anyway since his mother's not a fruitcake. Iris doesn't work hard, but she looks good, which is what matters, and her tits aren't saggy like Nora's. Her ass did fall, sure – but from heaven, the father thought, laughing quietly to himself at the joke he'd heard not long ago from his lawyer friend and thought was hilarious.

That's what the hotel maids are for: sweeping and making beds while Iris sits back in her rocking chair, painting her nails red. She eats a lot and doesn't exercise, and if she keeps that up she's not going to be curvy anymore – she'll just be fat. We had to call the doctor to prescribe

Nora some sedatives when Iris showed up with the boy, but I'm flesh-and-blood and in fine health. I can't just go and let myself be buried alive with a crazy woman the way these two nitwits probably wanted. It's no good for a man to be alone, much less for him to spend his life with a nutjob. I take care of her and all, but I can't just stop living, and once you're my age, you don't have the patience to go around visiting hookers; you need someone by your side, in your own bed, at all times, so things can happen on their own schedule. You have to be firm with crazy people, says I, or they'll never let you live your own life, which is something these two have never understood.

A large flock of small birds crossed in front of the boat, compact and skimming just above the water, like a single dark living creature. *Look at that, look at that,* thought the father, who had been sitting on the fore bench with the wind in his face. Then the blue shadow of the little island appeared, shimmering above the turquoise water, a shadow that gradually grew denser, took shape, became solid, and finally became unmistakably visible, with its details of seabirds and palm trees. Behind them, the turquoise contrasted with the gray-almost-black of the storm and created a sharply defined dark green line of separation along the horizon.

I'm not religious and I don't go to mass or any of that crap, but I do believe in God. How else do you explain this? The only thing greater than a man is God Himself, not some archbishop or arch-arch-bishop who pisses and shits like anybody else. You don't need priests or churches to see what I'm seeing. The twins were great at Manny's age – I baptized them myself, in the ocean. I got up early and walked into the water at six a.m. with one under each arm, both of them buck naked, barely three months old. I bathed them, dipped them under, and they bawled at the top of their lungs, I offered them to God, and, ta-da, they were baptized.

2:00 p.m.
Mario kept his eyes on Javier, who was jogging off, shirtless and in shorts, down the path into the mangrove swamp. They'd come ashore on a small coral-sand beach that hollowed out a gap in the mangroves. The father sat down on a trunk to stare at the sea and wait. Mario, scowling, remained standing beside the boat.

High above them, dozens of swallow-tailed kites soared in solemn circles the way carrion birds do on land. On the beach, at the edge of the mangroves, was a towering heap of conch shells as big as melons, the orange hue of their interiors muted by time. In the shade of the mangroves glowed the blue of discarded plastic bags. Near the beach, the water was light green and crystal-clear, and the sun shone blindingly on its ripples and flecks of foam and on the crushed-coral sand. But bitterness made

Mario indifferent to the beauty around him. *My life's pathetic, man. I get to sit around watching my asshole father*, he thought. *I should have gone to buy the beer. Look at him, sitting there oblivious – I could conk him on the back of the head with an oar and that would be the end of it.* Unsettled by the thought and hoping to elude the pang of his guilty conscience, the twin went to the boat to fetch some bait and one of his fishing lines. He walked about twenty meters almost knee-deep in the surf, parallel to the beach, which at that point was overgrown with mangroves. And there, his father now out of sight, he baited the hook, whirled the line in the air, and cast it fifteen meters out, skillfully, since he'd been performing that movement since he was a kid, and started to reel it back in. Mario preferred using the wooden rod on the beach; on the boat he used cane. The island was a good place to catch small snapper, parrotfish, and black margate. Mario was a decent beach fisherman, but when he still hadn't caught anything after a long while, he rolled up his line and walked toward the boat. The father was sitting in the same spot, furious at how long Javier was taking. Mario placed the rod in the boat and stood staring at the sand.

"What were you doing, jerking off or something? Mario was about to go looking for you. Christ, I don't know which of you is the bigger pain in the ass!" said the father when Javier emerged from the mangroves carrying a basket of beer bottles that clinked with every step. He'd run into his friends from Bogotá, Javier explained to Mario, not his father, whom he didn't even glance at.

Mario started up the boat again and took it out into open water. He accelerated hard so the boat reared up and the father, having stood up to retrieve a beer, almost lost his footing. Mario saw him miraculously regain his balance and heard him curse there amid the full glory of the sea. *Damn, so close,* he thought, and laughed silently to think he'd almost managed to make his father topple backward, like in a Condorito comic strip, and maybe even hit his head or fall into the water. The boat smacked the surface of the water three more times, and each time his father cursed. *Let's see what the old fart does now*, thought Mario, ready to gun the motor if his father tried to get up and come over to slap him.

Javier asked him what the hell he was doing, and Mario apologized. He'd gotten distracted, he said. Javier told him that was how people got killed at sea, and Mario said, "I said I was sorry. What more do you want? Want me to stop steering and get down on my knees?"

"There's a mark for every shark," the father said from the prow.

The storm seemed to be static, but raging. After swallowing most of the coast, it stopped, still very far away, locked up in its fury. It wasn't expanding, but its grays contrasted more and more intensely with the green of the sea, and the dark blue line separating the gray-almost-black from the turquoise was becoming more sharply defined. Mario was sure that the people on the island had told Javier it was foolish to go out in these conditions and Javier had chosen not to say anything to his brother and father. *And he's right. What's the point?* Mario thought. *The King's going to insist on going out anyway, no matter what. And it makes no difference to me. If we drown, we drown – no great loss. Though I do feel bad about Javier. And our crazy mother.*

For a while the only sounds they heard were the motor and the monotonous thudding of the hull against the waves. Mario stopped thinking about his father and for a very long, mercifully long, time he became one with the boat, with the motor and the sea, and took a break from being Mario. Then the motor coughed twice and recovered. It coughed again and cut off.

"Carburetor," said Javier.

On engine-powered vessels – ocean liners and thirty-foot fishing boats alike – a feeling of powerlessness descends immediately when the motor goes out. Even the smallest ripple jostles the hull, and life's true proportions are reestablished. The vessel's power on the water is revealed to be an illusion, and all that remains is its inert arrogance. Fear of thirst, sun, and hunger emerges: fear of death.

He's glaring at me like I shut it off on purpose, thought Mario, who was happy about the situation, since if there was any area in which he surpassed his father it was in his knowledge of outboard motors. *Now he's going to ask me why it went out when it's almost new.*

"Goddamn practically brand-new motor," the father said in his rough Antioquian accent, which contrasted with his sons' gentle coastal speech.

The twin knew his father was clueless, totally inept when it came to motors. The disgust he felt at the engine grease was visible a mile off, the way he tried to avoid getting it on his hands, which, though they were strong, hairy, tough, had lately been too well taken care of, now manicured by Iris, his new younger wife – the fingernails of a flirty old man, a lecherous old man, a disgraceful old man, Mario thought. Just to annoy him, he decided to take his time fixing the motor, which, as Javier had said, had gone out because some gunk was blocking the flow of the gasoline.

Mario knew he had his father by the balls.

Now that they weren't moving, the sun pounded them like

a battering ram. Mario disassembled the motor while Javier and the father portioned out lunch. Javier set a plate down on the bench next to his brother, but Mario didn't even look at him. The rice and beans were aglow in the bright tropical sun. Mario removed little parts and arranged them neatly, like pieces of jewelry, on a red chamois he had spread out on the bench, and from time to time he picked up the plate and took a few bites. The sea rippled gently, dazzling. Mario was all too familiar with the way his father ate when he was in a foul mood. He chewed quickly and eyed his food contemptuously, as if he were doing it a favor by eating it. Mario knew all of his father's facial expressions by heart.

"Do you have to take apart that whole thing?" Javier asked.

"What do you think?"

"You're going to take apart the whole motor?"

"You want to fix it, then?"

"No, no, no. Keep going."

"It looks pretty bad," Mario said, studying the motor. He glanced up at the sea. "And there's a current, so we're going to end up drifting if we can't get it started. And the sea's not looking good."

Nobody mentioned death but there it was, decked out in hood, cape, and scythe, perched on one of the benches.

"Pretty bad, my ass," said the father. "You just get it running, you hear me?"

"Your wish is my command, Your Majesty," the twin muttered, removing another part.

The jewels multiplied on the chamois. Mario blew on parts, rinsed them in fresh water, held them up toward the sun and squinted at them, rinsed them with gasoline, dried them with a rag, blew and looked again. *I can make sure we all drown if I feel like it, you miserable old bastard. Either that or die of thirst*, he thought. Half of the motor gleamed in pieces on the bench, and the other half was a carapace full of bones. Mario realized his father was observing his skill with fascination and involuntary admiration.

The old bastard's already having some doubts, he thought, ecstatic.

3:00 p.m.

"A wave always arrives at its destination, and it always starts out from its place of origin," says the mother as if she were describing in detail, rather than prophesying, an imminent event. "Same with the wind. Wave and wind. Human heart."

She'd gone to the kitchen looking for lunch and sat down at

the table with the members of her retinue. The neckbone of the chicken was dissolving in her mouth, and the cook warned her, or maybe it was her conscience, to be careful not to choke on a vertebra or on the head either, which was watching her with curious, mocking eyes. A breeze blew through the restaurant. The succulent yam split open under her fork like a hot iceberg.

"And the plantain. Look! The plantain!" she said.

"Motorboat, motorboat becalmed in its solitude," the throng chorused in response, reminding her of the existence of the father, her husband, the King, whom Nora had forgotten while she slurped the chicken head and sliced the yam with her fork.

"Oh, yes, oh!" replied the mother, Queen of Persia and Playamar, saying "oh" again and again until the cook came over to see what was going on.

"May God forgive him for his wickedness, and forgive them if they end up doing what the sea suggests!"

"You shouldn't talk like that, Doña Nora, no, no," advised the cook, who was black, born and raised in Santiago de Tolú. She had an age-old sadness in her eyes and smile and, on top of the sadness, joy.

"Oh dear, what are we going to do, Cordelia!" Nora said.

"Imogenia. Don't shout, you'll frighten the angels. Cordelia's my cousin, remember? She helps out on Sundays. She lives in Múcura."

Nora wasn't sure the cook had actually mentioned angels, and this uncertainty provoked a twinge of terror. "Names, names, what do names matter?" she said hastily. "Go on, Imogenia, go get me a little more sancocho, but don't tell *Him* – he'll kill me."

"*Him!*" cried the throng in the distance, startling her.

They'd all headed off toward the beach to sing with the waves in the background, which had grown larger and filled near to bursting with light. "*Him* who caused so much pain. *Him* who is killing her, has killed her, will kill her," the throng cried, and boom, the wave fell, opening up its fans across the sand, *ushhhhh*, like labyrinths of the soul. Nora heard every detail of its sandy seepings and tiny eddies, like those of sadness. And the sea stretched out at their feet, slowly, with all its lugubrious bolts of imperial silk.

"Sea that grows shadowy with my love," said Nora as sturdy Imogenia grew progressively smaller and more compassionate, as if she were moving away through the eyepiece of a telescope or through the tunnel of death.

Imogenia returned. She was actually part of the plot the death squads were cooking up against Nora with her husband's help, and she wasn't the least bit compassionate, or at least not a reliable bit, and the treacherous cook was coming with the bowl of sancocho, accompanied by her husband, who was black with powerful arms, arms that could at any moment, together with Imogenia's, tie her to the bed the way you would a goat. Nora knew the King had instructed them to tie her down and summon a nurse from a luxury hotel twenty minutes away to sedate her. That could happen any time the boys weren't around – they never would have put up with it and would have stood up to their father and cut the slave's throat to keep him from tying her up and poisoning her with sedatives or giving her electroshocks, as had happened a few times before.

"Everything all right, Doña Nora?" inquired the black man, who looked like a prince in his arrogance and elegant clothing.

"If it weren't for the hatred and resentment in your eyes that expose you as a slave, you would have had me fooled!" Nora said, and let out a gale of laughter that revealed the pink gaps of several missing incisors and the blackness of her molars.

"Calm down now, Doña Nora, or I've got the strap and the syringe over there," the evil black man replied. When her boys were around (not the husband, whose most obsequious slave he was), the scoundrel was more careful about the way he talked to her.

"Don't talk like that, don't be cruel – you get her even more upset. I shouldn't have asked you to come!" Imogenia said.

Nora didn't feel like answering and turned back to her sancocho. If she wanted to save her own life and thereby secure the future of the human race, she was going to have to be cunning and trick them. She didn't even try to protest or insult them, fearing they'd take advantage of the commotion to swipe a piece of manioc from her plate. Cunning, more cunning, endless cunning was what Nora needed in order to defeat them. Her sons would come back to avenge her and the blood would flow on the beaches.

"Debacle," said Nora with her mouth full.

"What did you say?" Imogenia asked.

When Nora looked up she realized Imogenia's husband wasn't there anymore. Her eyes were exhausted from having the glow of so many worlds, some of them friendly, many of them razor-sharp, crammed inside them.

"She'd like to take a nap," she said.

"Who?"

"The queen of Persia. Sahamarakahanda V."

"The fifth?" asked the husband, who'd been hiding in the thatch of the roof like a bat.

"Hush, devil-man. Get out of here," said Imogenia. "Go on and finish your sancocho, Doña Nora. Did you like it?"

"She liked it," Nora answered. "But it could have used some avocado."

"And what is Queen Saharawhatthehellever going to do with that avocado, if I may ask?" said the husband, and Imogenia told him that if he didn't leave right now she would chase him out with a broom. The husband skulked out with his tail between his legs, and this time he didn't even attempt to fly up and hide in the roof of the restaurant, the damn vampire.

"That's how you expel demons and cockroaches," said Nora, who was almost ready to trust Imogenia again.

As the cook and Nora walked toward the bungalow, the swallow-tailed kites wheeled there at the far edge of the sky, and the waves rolled in with the enormous power and brightness of that time of day. Some cold bells took flight, startling Nora, as if she had climbed up a medieval cathedral and squatted down to urinate in the bell tower. Then they stopped ringing and went quiet. Everything returned to the tropics and the glare of the tropical sea, and she realized that today she'd have the opportunity to resolve the issue of the cook once and for all. With Imogenia dead, exterminating the husband would be child's play, and that hussy Carlota and the gaggle of gossips with their rotten phalluses who'd tormented her so grievously would fall alongside him.

It would be today, but not right now. Right now she was sleepy and little inclined to embark on matters having to do with the common good. They would understand the situation at the ministry, since they were familiar with her legendary efficiency and diligence. The important thing was that she suspect nothing, the whore. That she believe she loved her. And when she came into the bungalow now, Nora should take care not to look at a particular plank in the ceiling, where the blunt instrument of justice and redemption was hidden. Imogenia would die. Iris, the placid concubine, would die. The boy would live. Imogenia's toad of a husband would die.

"Splendor of the afternoon," sang the chorus of the virtuous, now packed in behind the shower curtain, egging her on. "Vengeance that will come without warning, a swell and surge in his throat. Scattered brains, spattered blood can be auspicious. Discord."

"Exactly. Completely mistaken. Thank you, boys."

"Shall I turn on the air conditioner, Doña Nora?"

The cool air blew across Nora's sweaty forehead, bringing profound relief. She lay down on the bed and stared up at the planks of the ceiling, except for one in particular, and she forgot about the cook, who covered her with a white sheet that Nora pushed away.

"The flies are going to bother you."

"Just sleep," Nora said.

"Do you want me to send over one of the girls to give you a bath?"

Nora shook her head and removed her slip.

"If you're going to get undressed, I'm going to cover you up."

She placed the sheet over her and Nora flung it off again. The air conditioner purified the tense room. The mother slipped into the fathomless sleep of the mad while outside the bungalow the grackles piercingly expressed their thoughts in the almond trees and coconut palms.

4:00 p.m.

Javier saw his brother take apart almost the entire motor, put it back together, fail to start it, and start taking it apart again. They were floating adrift, the islands gradually fading from view.

Without a motor, the current would carry them inexorably out to sea.

I can't believe this shit is too much for you, Javier almost said, but he kept quiet so as not to set his father off.

"Weren't you supposed to be the genius at this kind of thing?" the father asked suddenly, his voice heavy with contempt. "He's all jingle and no popsicle, this kid."

Javier saw death in his brother's screwdriver and went to grab him and hold him back if need be. But Mario just blew on another engine part without looking at anybody, not even the sea, and kept removing more and more parts. Javier sat down across from him on the bench, his back to the father.

"Is it going to start?" he asked.

"It's going to start. They haven't made a motor that's bested me yet. But it'll start when I feel like it."

"Smartass, like everybody around here," said the father with a primordial disdain for the high-spirited and minimally violent nature of the coastal people.

"Or he can come over and start it himself – I'll wait."

"Shut up, shut up, asshole," Javier said in a low voice, close to losing his temper. "Fix that shit and shut up."

After a while, when he felt like it, Mario started the motor. He revved it and made the boat rear up so it slapped against the water a few times, but the father was braced and didn't fall. *He must be going crazy too*, thought Javier. When the slapping became less intense, Javier avoided looking up so as not to see the expression on his father's face. Twenty minutes later the father said, "Here," and when it seemed like Mario wasn't going to stop, Javier leaped up, shoved him gently out of the way, and shut off the motor.

"Cut it out. It's not right, it's not right," he muttered, looking at the floor of the boat, where countless fish – colorful, cold, slimy, sharp, their mouths opening and closing – flopped ankle-deep.

"We're not going to catch shit here," said Mario, also in a low voice.

"You looking to get smacked?"

"Let him just try it!" said Mario. He'd left the screwdriver within reach, on the platform where the motor was strapped down.

"If he doesn't smack you, I will."

At first Javier thought his brother was wrong, since they managed to catch a few medium-size mojarras and a king mackerel that weighed almost four pounds, but then the fish just stopped biting. And he was happy when they did. *Can't give the old man the satisfaction, even if it means we have to keep sitting here without a nibble.* The sea had grown agitated. At any moment, the grays of the far-off storm might burst from their confines and the torrent of rain, wind, and lightning bear down on them. Javier decided not to smoke any more marijuana until they were back from fishing. *Now's not the time, especially with these two assholes and their death wishes. I've never seen Mario like that, and the old man had better watch out or he's going to get stabbed with a goddamn screwdriver. It might do him some good, actually – maybe he'd learn some respect*, he thought, and took a deep breath to keep his blood from boiling too. Since the fish weren't biting, Javier idly watched the storm. It looked close, but though the lightning was intense, the thunder was still taking a while to reach them. Yet it could change directions at any moment, and if it turned south, they wouldn't have time to escape. He mentioned it to his father, who didn't answer. Mario, for his part, muttered something Javier didn't quite catch, though he imagined, knowing his brother, it was probably something about how it'd be a good thing if the sea swallowed them up and this shitty world came to an end once and for all.

Javier was exasperated by Mario's endless whining about how he'd never asked to be alive and it would have been better if he'd never been born. He was always tempted to retort that a person didn't get to ask to be alive or not, don't be a pussy – you get life, and then it's your business if you shoot yourself or stick your fucking head in the toilet, nobody gives a shit. He had to bite his tongue, especially since, when he was drinking, after a certain point Javier would get more and more worked up, and two or three times he'd ended up punching or slapping Mario in a drunken fury and then felt bad about it afterward.

On the western horizon, to the right of the stone-colored storm, the sky was turning gold and pink, presaging an intensely glowing sunset. Javier was tempted to dig around in his bag for his pipe, but he refrained. Things might seem calm now, but everybody in the boat, himself included, was tense with worry, and arrogance, and uncertainty, and disdain, all of that combined, and somebody had to keep his head together as much as possible. Javier was willing to kill for his brother, even if he sometimes lost his temper and struck him, just as he was willing to kill for his mother.

He used his knife to cut open one of the large king mackerel, plunged his hand into its cold belly, and pulled it out again full of dripping guts and glands, which he tossed into the sea. When he finished cleaning the mackerel, he continued with one of the crevalle jacks. The smell was searing in his nostrils. Once they'd been cleaned, Javier put the fish in the coolers, where the ice was already half melted. Every once in a while, he pulled his lines out of the water to check the bait and then cast them again. The fish still weren't biting. Sometimes he changed the bait out for no reason. Mario and the father did the same. The image of the murderous king, the main character in the book he was reading these days, kept turning over in Javier's mind, while the light and the colors of the twilight blended together in a world now completely empty of boats and birds. He stood up and stretched. Before sitting again, he leaned over the edge of the boat and, thirty feet below, saw the dark shadow of the corals and aquatic plants in the water, which was still blue and luminous.

Too bad, he thought. *A couple tokes of weed would have been awesome. No wonder that one guy spends all his time painting watercolors, so many of them he's going to run out of paper even though he brought an entire suitcase of the stuff. And his wife isn't bad. That's the good thing about the coast – there are plenty of women around during the tourist season. A man doesn't get bored, and sometimes you can even pick one up. Or at least talk with one. The days stretch out endless during the low season, though books help. It was nice of him to bring me books. Of course, I drove the three of them all the way from Montería in the jeep and charged them cheap. Though it wasn't free either. You can't go around giving away your time and labor, no matter how good of friends they are or how many favors they've done for you.*

Still wearing his clip-on sunglasses even though the sun was setting, he looked indifferently at his father, who was scowling as he held his rod, unwilling to give up even though no fish were biting. The admiration Javier had once felt for him – the only form of love the old man really made possible – had long since disappeared. Absolute power may dazzle a child, but not a young man. *I'm not letting anybody fuck with me ever again if I can help it,* he thought as he reeled in one of the lines to check whether the bait was still intact. *He's going to have to show me some respect, and Mario too. We're not asking for money – we can earn that ourselves. And if he demands the bungalows back, we'll pack up our things and take our nutcase mother to live somewhere else. But he won't do it, because then he'd have to run the restaurant himself, and he doesn't have the patience to go around tracking the sugar and oil stocks, and without that it won't stay afloat. You can't turn a profit in a restaurant if you don't keep an eye on the little things. Employees will steal anything, even toilet paper if you're not careful. Not to mention the quality issue – who knows what kind of crap they'll serve to tourists when he's in charge. The old man doesn't care, and the cook takes off whenever she wants and makes another employee fill in. The guests eat whatever you give them – what else can they do? – rubbery fish and tough manioc, and they rarely complain. I'm not saying it has to be a sixteen-star place, but the manioc should at least be edible, damn it. And sometimes there's fresh fish but for whatever reason they fry up frozen stuff, I'm sure of it.*

The sun kept setting, and the horizon filled up with color. Apart from that, nothing seemed to change with the passing of time – the storm's contours remained steady, as if it were a solid mass, and the sea birds were still absent, and the water continued its imperturbable rippling. But at any moment chaos was going to break out all around them, like smoke, like lava. From what he'd seen in his twenty-six years, and also from what he'd read, Javier tended to think life consisted of continually entering hell and then exiting it again. Which didn't at all mean you might as well kill yourself, like that pussy Mario thought.

Nothing of the sort.

A person has to live happiness to the fullest when it comes, even if it's just for a little while, especially during childhood. Even he and Mario, despite all the chaos, had experienced it. Hadn't they? That's why the good moments had been so intense, Javier thought. And because they'd been so intense, you had to conclude that a person was obliged to live all of life, whatever it brought. That's why he got so pissed off when his brother expressed his childish desire to die. You had to respect life, damn it, and Javier had no patience for complaining or recriminations against God, whether from his brother, himself, or anybody else.

And what was Mario complaining about anyway? Didn't Javier see him having a good time with the boat and the motor and the lines and hooks, and completely forgetting, if only for a little while, about suicide and blaming God?

Look, look at that sunset! he thought then, as if the orange on the horizon were presenting the conclusive argument against his brother's darkness, his own darkness, and even the cruel and involuntary darkness of the madwoman back on shore.

5:00 p.m.

My name is Ligia María Zuluaga, I'm in fourth grade at the Colegio María Auxiliadora, and I live in La Floresta, Medellín, Antioquia, Colombia, South America, the Americas, Earth, the Milky Way, the Universe. I thought the ocean was so pretty. Those sunsets, just gorgeous. We came on vacation from Medellín in my father's jeep, and when we got to Tolú and I saw that huge, blue, blue enormousness that you could see – you know? – at the ends of the streets, it sort of gave me a jolt and I almost started crying. My daddy has three taxis that my uncles drive for him and an eighteen-wheeler. It gave my mommy a jolt too. My two little sisters were sleepy, silly things, and looked at the sea with their eyelids drooping and didn't see anything.

I've had so much fun here!

We came to a hotel that's named Cabañas Playamar because the bungalows are by the sea and there's lots of sand. There are lots of kids, and I made friends with them. Last night like a hundred of us from all the bungalows went out with a flashlight to shine it on the crabs and chase after them on the beach. Some of the boys killed them with sticks, poor things – none of us girls did. We're going to go out tonight too, but they're saying the sea is going to get real rough so we can't go swimming, but I'm scared to get in the water at night anyways because I'm afraid a fish will bite me, or a barracuda. The water is warmer than the outdoors.

We've had a good time, but my mommy told my daddy he couldn't keep staying up all night with the man from the hotel and doing so-called business deals. My mommy says she's getting fed up because we came here to rest, not to fool around or get drunk. Of course, the man from the hotel isn't here today because he went fishing with his sons. The cook says they're going to drown. The lady from the hotel is crazy and goes around in a slip and my mommy says poor thing because sometimes at night she screams and he goes and gives her a shot to make her be quiet, the cook's children told me. They're blackest black and they know how to play with tree trunks in the ocean. Here on the coast there's lots of different fruits. There's watermelons, mangos, papayas, melons, and loquats too, but different from the ones in Medellín. My mommy says they're really gritty, but I love them, though they do stain your clothes.

Everything's just so so so pretty!

I like fried fish. My favorite kind is called lane snapper, which is small and red. I always tell the cook, "I'd like a lane snapper, if there are any!" She always says look how this little blond girl wolfs food down, it's like she's been out in the fields all day. The cook comes over to talk to my mommy, and my mommy doesn't like it because she hates gossip, but she's not sure how to get away. The cook says the owner has made life really hard for the crazy lady. The cook is fat, but I like her because she braided my hair with beads and says the beads look really pretty with my blond hair and my eyes because they're green. But I don't like people telling me I have green eyes all the time, it's so boring. We've had such a good time on this vacation. Yesterday we drove to Tolú and visited the church…

I'm Yónatan, the eight-year-old boy who goes to the Escuela Fernando González in Envigado, but I don't live in town, I live on a farm up in the hills, and I walk down to school like twenty minutes every day. I'm the one the twin gave the money to, the bill all tattered and stinky, and it ended up falling apart afterward. Us kids don't like that twin because he's always mad. But Javier's cool, all the kids say so, and he plays soccer with us on the beach. I was supposed to do some homework on my vacation, but I haven't started yet. Why do they give us homework when we're on vacation? Or why do they call it vacation then?

When I told my grandma about the money and how the twin never paid attention to us kids, she said, "Poor thing, the boy's had a rough time of it." My grandma is Doña Libe, and we live in my grandparents' bungalows that are down past Playamar. She said, "But if he messes with any of you, I won't be held responsible for my actions." On vacation my aunts and uncles come with their children so there are like fifteen of us cousins. Almost all of them live in Medellín, except my aunt, who lives in La Estrella. They put all of us boys in one room and all the girls in another with lots of bunk beds and in the boys' room we have lots of fun turning on the flashlights at night and farting. "You're so gross!" the girls yell at us from their room, and we laugh. We have so much fun!

And I'm the tourist who had his first shots of aguardiente at nine in the morning, after a breakfast of corn bollos and eggs at the hotel restaurant, and who's been drinking ever since. Today, though, I'm taking it slow so I don't get blackout drunk and start wandering down the beaches like a zombie.

"Juan Carlos, you've got to watch that drinking, man," Javier, the twin, who's a friend of mine, told me one day.

What had happened was I'd fallen asleep on the beach down there where the huts with the food and dancing are. Other guests went to let him know, and Javier sent some people to get me and carry me to my room. But luckily I'd already woken up and they didn't have to carry me.

"Something could happen to you, dude – you could get robbed or killed. Things are pretty quiet around here, but you never know."

And he's right. Especially in my case, since I came here alone and who's going to ask after me. Javier's a good guy. I'm going to go sit on that tree trunk and watch the sun set.

My name is Johanna. I came with Ricardo, my boyfriend, who'd promised to take me to Cartagena, but he couldn't afford it – Cartagena's for the jet set, he says, he'll never be able to afford it – so here we are. Ricardo wanted me to put on a happy face, since he says this wasn't cheap either, the flights from Bogotá and everything, but how could I? I mean, this place is packed.

Since everything was full, they put us in the bungalow beside the owner's wife, who goes around all day in a slip, sometimes stark naked until they force her to put clothes on, and sometimes she starts talking and shouting in the middle of the night. Yesterday this drunk guy was blasting cantina music practically all night in one of the other bungalows, and I couldn't get to sleep. It's all really weird, because the owner, who's like seventy years old, has a girlfriend, a much younger woman with a little baby. Everything here on the coast is weird. So different! He's also got twin sons. They're handsome, especially the one with light-colored eyes, very much my taste. All tanned and wiry and with blond curls. Golden boy. Ricardo was really pale and made the mistake of staying in the water a really long time and got totally sunburned – even the sheet against his skin makes him cry out, so now he's in the bedroom with a fever and milk of magnesia smeared all over him, and I have to be out here on my own, entertaining myself as best I can. If the owner's son hadn't gone off fishing with his dad and brother, I'd have at least been able to talk to him.

But no, and now I've got to come down to walk on the beach alone where there aren't so many people playing with beach balls, children crying and shrieking, or men drinking aguardiente. The cook recommended I come here in front of the airport, where it's quieter. And it is. It's definitely quiet and pretty in this area. Not for swimming, since I'm terrified of jellyfish, but for walking . . . Look at that! Just look at that sunset! Poor Ricardo's really missing out. The sea is so beautiful!

6:00 p.m.

The father had looked at the sunset without wanting to make too much of it. Today's had been so striking, though, that he gazed at it a couple of seconds longer than he usually did at those postcard-worthy sunsets the tourists got so excited about. When he was drinking with his guests, he'd of course join them in watching the setting sun and even wax poetic, but in such situations his lyricism had a touristic, professional quality, quite different from his proud and intimate relationship with the sea. And if it weren't bad for business, on more than one occasion when the guests were going on and on about some everyday, run-of-the-mill sunset, he would have told them, "After a while around these parts, a man gets tired of watching so many goddamn sunsets, believe me."

The heat had diminished as the evening advanced. Feeling less suffocated by the sun, the father took the reins again. In his immense self-confidence, he noticed but then dismissed as inconsequential the way Mario had cranked the boat's motor and at one point had clenched the screwdriver in his fist. He thought he understood how his sons thought, so he never felt fear, not even now that he was at a clear disadvantage, since any strength the two of them had was thanks to him – otherwise they would have been as helpless as their mother. And if Javier thought he was going to intimidate him with his books, he had another think coming. The father felt some pride in his son's intellectual capacities and even bragged about them – if he'd been drinking and Javier wasn't around, he'd go to the young man's bungalow and show a tourist the piles of books – but he also despised them.

The sun set and deep twilight fell.

"Get that shit running so we can start fishing for real," he said.

Mario turned on the motor and started the boat moving smoothly through the water, as if he'd lost his nerve or as if, at the last minute, they'd declared a truce and rationality now held sway once more. The father and Javier started organizing everything so they wouldn't have to fumble around in the dark for the wire cutters or the tackle box, or turn on the flashlights to find them and scare the fish away. From time to time the father would stare intently at the water, looking for the best place to drop anchor. Only once did he glance at Mario out of the corner of his eye; the twin was frowning at the steering arm and following his instructions without saying a word. *Good choice*, he thought. *The more defiant he is, the worse it'll be for him.*

The water was starting to turn dark blue in its swift transition to blackness.

"Here it is," he said.

Mario shut off the motor, they dropped anchor, and the father instructed Javier to serve the food. They ate beans and rice in silence. The father looked out at the sea as he chewed; his sons looked down at their plates or the bottom of the boat. He asked Javier to pass him a Coca-Cola and drank it in large gulps after wiping the mouth of the bottle with his hand.

Fishermen freaking out about the slightest hint of a breeze, he thought. *They make up excuses not to go out and then go around complaining about how poor they are. That's what I'm always telling them: you assholes were born in a goddamn cornucopia. All you have to do is go out and catch a fish and come back home to fry it up and eat it. Coconuts fall out of the palm trees right on your damn head. Plantains and rice are super cheap. But these lazy blacks can't even do that, and then they kick up a fuss when a man goes out fishing when there's a storm somewhere, even if it's practically all the way in La Guajira or goddamn Venezuela. And then their kids go hungry and their bellies swell up and everything.*

"Pour the coffee, would you?" he told Mario.

Deep twilight turned to night. The sky filled with stars. Lightning was still flashing at the edges of the storm, but the thunder had stopped rumbling, as if the storm was moving farther away. After coffee, they baited and cast their lines. The father wasn't expecting the first bite to be so aggressive, nor that it would come almost as soon as the line hit the water. As he yanked on the rod to lodge the hook firmly in the bony, almost rock-hard, mouth of the tarpon – he could tell immediately what kind of fish it was – he stumbled and twisted his ankle, which made him curse loudly. Javier grabbed the rod and started fighting with the fish as it tried to escape, leaping and gleaming not just silver but phosphorescent and fantastical some twenty meters from the boat. Much more real than the tarpon itself in the shadows of evening was the din it made as it crashed back into the water. The father's cries of pain suddenly ceased, and the world was filled only with the struggle with the fish.

"Let out the line a little, don't pull," said Mario. "He could snap it. Let him wear himself out. Just let him wear himself out."

The father turned on the flashlight, examined his foot, and decided his ankle wasn't broken, though the sprain hurt as much as a break. *It's going to swell up like crazy*, he thought. The fish leaped again and plunged into the water, and the father guessed it weighed at least a hundred and seventy-five pounds. All at once he realized they were surrounded by a huge school of tarpon. He could sense their presence by the sound of their fins gently beating under the water and the murmur they made when they came to the surface for oxygen. In his excitement, he nearly forgot about the pain. He felt a nibble on another line and gave a sharp pull to hook the fish. He applied the brake mechanism to the reel, which stopped screeching, and the tarpon rose up in the deep darkness and crashed back down again some fifteen meters from the boat. Whenever the father moved, the pain in his ankle would flare up again and make him cry out, while Javier was going from one side of the boat to the other as the fish dashed back and forth.

"Don't reel him in," Mario told his brother, who had to move quickly to keep up with the fish's rapid circular path. The father turned on the flashlight again and shone it on Mario. The twin had started the motor and was ready to follow the fish with the boat so they wouldn't have to give it too much line.

"What are you doing, moron?" the father yelled, but Mario seemed not to hear him. "Can't you see I hurt my ankle? Come grab this shit, will you?"

"Shut off the motor, shut it off, shut it off," said Javier, giving the fish some more line. The father was convinced Mario was just pretending to help his brother in order to sabotage the father, taking advantage of the fact that he was weak and battling both pain and the huge fish. Mario shut off the motor.

"Go and help him," Javier said.

Agilely, Mario clambered toward the father, snatched the fishing rod, and, still holding it, shoved him in the chest so the older man fell back on his rump on the cushion of fish and felt the pain shoot through his ankle. It took the father a few seconds to process what had happened. He'd have liked to beat his son to death, but he barely had the strength to get up from the bottom of the boat and go over to sit on his bench again, wordlessly, like an old man. The pain was intense, and as the twins fought with the tarpon, the father felt the chill of night coming on. He'd brought a nylon jacket, but his backpack was in the compartment in the bow and there was no way he could get to it since his ankle couldn't bear his weight. Their hands full, his sons couldn't help him either. *Fucking Mario wouldn't pass it to me anyway*, he thought, suddenly remembering the shove he'd already forgotten, maybe because it was so ludicrous. He took off his soaked shirt, wrung it out, and began to shiver. His ankle started swelling. His anger surged again and turned cold. He turned on the flashlight, then pulled ice cubes out of the cooler and put them on his ankle. He tore up the T-shirt and bandaged the ankle to see if that would brace it and allow him to stand. Painfully, he tottered to his feet and promptly sat back down. The two fish were leaping, struggling to escape, closer to the boat, but now, with the darkness falling, their gleam in the air was only imaginary. The father thought he'd better watch out for his ankle when Mario or Javier pulled the tarpon into the boat, since he'd have to help them with the hook, and one blow from the fish's tail could crush his ankle and leave him completely helpless. Sitting on the bench, he lifted his bandaged foot and placed it in the ice chest until it started to hurt too much and he pulled it back out. Every once in a while, he'd submerge it again. *You're going to get what's coming to you, assholes*, he thought. The sentence was directed at everything that was not himself: his sons, the fish, his ankle, the distant storm, even God.

The storm was moving away but also intensifying. Streaks of lightning flashed at its edges with horizontal and vertical branches and tentacles, while a formless glow flickered within it, illuminating an enclosed inferno of lightning, rain, and wind.

The storm occupied one corner of the universe. Everything else seemed tranquil and faintly undimmed by vestiges of light.

Mario was aware that when he lifted the tarpon into the boat
he'd get another chance to shove his father in the darkness. He
remembered the hook and wondered whether the old man,
frenzied with pain, might be capable of turning it against him.
But he was determined. From time to time, out of the corner
of his eye, he would glance at Javier, who had worked the fish
effectively and now had it under control and ready to reel in to
the side of the boat. The father had come over with the hook
to help him pull it out of the water, and for an instant Mario
thought that Javier, too, was thinking of shoving him. Then his
brother said curtly, "Cut the crap."

Javier had guessed at his brother's intention to injure the
father further or even knock him overboard if it came to that.
So now he's defending the old bastard, Mario thought as he lowered
the rod after the tarpon's leap to keep the line from breaking
as the fish fell back into the water. The fish was a fighter, and the
twin had managed to bring it only a few meters closer. *Instead,
he should be taking the opportunity to teach him something he never
learned as a kid: to respect my mother, damn it, and treat people right.*
Mario had to make an effort not to haul on the fish too hard in
his rage and risk losing it.

Another fish bit and made the reel on the father's second rod shriek. Mario saw him turn on the flashlight, go over to the side, cut the line, and hobble back to Javier's bench. *When you want to catch them, they escape, and when you want them to escape, they end up getting hooked,* he thought. *Maybe it's for the best. The tourists don't like tarpon because it's so bony. They don't know how to eat it. The cook fries it and serves it with coconut sauce, which makes it seem less bony. When she puts her mind to it, it's the most delicious fish out there, but two of these giants is plenty. Jesus, this one's really got a yank in him!*

He'd abandoned his plan to shove the father again, since Javier was sure to intervene and he didn't want any trouble with his twin. They sometimes fought, as brothers do, but the bond between them was so strong that afterward they always felt terrible about it and tried to avoid fighting as much as possible. There were still many hours to go, and Mario would find another opportunity to get even. Stubborn as the father was, there was no way he was going to decide to turn back just because of a sprained ankle. *He'll want to keep going even if we end up having to saw his damn foot off when we get home,* Mario thought. *That's one thing about the old bastard – he won't back down from anything.*

"Hold on to it, I'm here," the father said.

As young boys, and even as teenagers, he used to bring them with him when he had to take care of anything at the banks in Montería or Sincelejo so they could see him dealing with money or filling out paperwork and learn a little something about it. The father strode unfazed through those intimidating, overly air-conditioned offices and spoke to the officers responsible for reviewing his loan applications as if he were their equal; they almost always approved him. And the boys came to recognize his superiority and perceive his pride at not ever having had to put on a necktie in order to be somebody, unlike the directors and assistant directors of those institutions, public and private alike, who were, he claimed, mere employees, grunts, stiffs, poor suckers.

Mario saw him grab the hook and, still half mad with pain, brace himself to haul the fish into the boat. The twin thought the ankle might be fractured and made an effort not to feel either compassion or distress at giving in to compassion, and focused on wearing out the tarpon with lateral tugs. It wasn't leaping anymore, but the fish still maintained a static, almost lifeless tension on the line, as if the hook had gotten caught on a coral reef.

As they landed the tarpon, which weighed more than two hundred pounds and was at least six feet long, Javier made his father lose his balance and fall back onto his rear end in the bottom of the boat with the hook and the fish. The father cried out in pain. The shove hadn't been intentional, Mario guessed, since the old man got to his feet again, cursing his ankle, and didn't yell at Javier or try to do anything to him. He stopped cursing once he reached the bench and, holding his ankle in his left hand, shone the flashlight on the tarpon, which was flopping in the bottom of the boat, metallic and radiant.

"Son of a bitch sure is gorgeous," he said.

During their childhood and into adolescence, the boys had admired the father's self-confidence, and even his ruthlessness. When he was confronted by the drunk he'd persuaded to sell him a jeep while on a bender – who turned out to be the son of a prominent politician and landowner from Montería – the father held his ground on the porch of his house in Playamar. He ended up convincing him that people are just as responsible for the things they do when they're sloshed as they are for those they do when they're thinking clearly. And he told him that nobody ever got anywhere going around moaning about their mistakes or being consumed with regret. It was best to just face things head on and take your losses. Pretty piddly losses, too, really, he added, since while he'd gotten the jeep for cheap, it had hardly been free. And throughout that conversation, which got tense at times when it looked like the landowner's son might resort to violence, he didn't tell the twins to leave, or admonish them that this was a conversation for grown-ups, because he wanted them to learn how men do business.

Mario's fish was getting weaker. It was no longer dashing or leaping. It had dived deeper and now, when he tugged on the line, it felt like he was uprooting a boulder from the ocean floor. Distracted by what had happened or, rather, not happened between Javier and the father, Mario's attention occasionally wandered, and he was lucky the line didn't break. Javier came up and gave him advice – "Keep working him, don't let him rest" – advice that was completely superfluous, since Mario knew exactly what he was doing. Out of the corner of his eye, he saw the father remove his bandage to examine his ankle and then put it back on. When the father said to pull harder, that he looked like a pussy, the twin's ire came flooding back.

"Screw you," he replied, though he wasn't sure his father heard him.

Javier did, though, and said quietly, "Just ignore him. Keep doing your thing."

As a vast spread of stars filled the part of the sky that wasn't blotchy with storm clouds, the father and sons seemed to become trapped in a deepening well. Mario battled with the fish while waves of resentment toward his father swept through him. He felt the tarpon's leaps through the rod. The beams of the flashlights illuminated the fish, and it floated suspended for a moment, like a moon, some twenty meters from the boat. It was even bigger than Javier's. Startled, Mario barely managed to lower the rod to keep the line from tensing and breaking when the fish plunged into the water again.

"This is going to take a while," Javier remarked.

The father said that if his ankle weren't busted to shit, he could land it in half an hour, forty-five minutes max. The boys pretended not to hear him.

"Shit," said Mario as he yanked on his rod. "He's got his second wind."

The fish had been able to rest while the twin was distracted by his hatred. *You can't give an inch or you have to start over from the beginning*, he thought. *It's crazy how they catch their breath and keep fighting. Old bastard. I hope his foot is fucking broken. But I doubt it. Look at him.* The father had turned on the flashlight and was using one of the oars as a crutch as he headed over to the tackle box, went back, and started tying the hook and sinker to the line he'd cut.

"It's flagging again," said Javier.

Mario fought another long hour with the fish and then, just as he was hauling it in, a second before Javier managed to snag it with the hook, the fishing line snapped and both the tension and the fish suddenly vanished. The father said:

"I knew you were going to let it get away."

"Shut up, damn it," said Javier.

8:00 p.m.

Nora was awakened by the noises of the long-snouted marsupial hiding in the ceiling – the instrument of her justice. The grackles had been quiet for a while, and the herons were no longer winging their way overhead toward the swamp. The world belonged to the bats and crabs once more.

"Wind," said Nora.

The air conditioning made her shiver.

"Wind," replied the chorus.

She didn't turn on the bedside lamp. One of the girls who worked in the kitchen knocked on the door, came in, and switched on the overhead light. Nora was naked.

"Turn it off," she said, and everybody corroborated her command. The girl turned it off.

"What would you like to eat, Doña Nora?" she asked. When Nora didn't answer, the girl said, "There's some leftover sea-bass sancocho."

"Yes."

"Should I turn off the air conditioning? Do you want a sheet?"

"Yes. No."

Fifty meters from the bungalow, the sea murmured. The throng, crammed in behind the shower curtain, had begun pointing out that when the time came, she was going to have to do the kangaroo with the hammer snout, the hammer with kangaroo ears. Brains. Audacity. Cracked skulls. Audacity, more audacity, endless audacity.

"Order in the court. The appeal is dismissed," said Nora in a loud, firm voice.

"What did you say, Doña Nora?"

"I didn't say anything, Doña Lora. But I did say something. Hee-hee-hee-hee."

She put on her slip and went out on the porch and down the steps to the strip of sparse lawn in front of the house. The stars seemed unsteady, as if at any moment a hand might sweep them away like a sand mandala. Nora knew about mandalas, Buddhism, and Tibetan monks. Her mother often told her she couldn't understand how Nora, who'd been such a hippie, had ended up marrying such a monster. Nora's mother, who was dead now, had been the principal of a girls' school in Cali. Nobody had loathed and despised the father more than her.

"Om, om, om!" Nora shouted at the top of her lungs, still gazing up at the stars.

The girl, perplexed by the sacred syllable, was unsure what to do.

"I'll bring you your food, then," she said finally, and practically ran off toward the kitchen.

The throng chanted:

"He wished to leave you deprived of both sky and firmament. To abandon you, live with her, and do away with your children."

"Yes, yes, yes! Oh yes, the bastard!"

"And now his servants will pay dearly for it, with their brains shattered, tattered, battered, spattered, scattered, splattered. And afterward the princes will grant him the sea as his tomb," the throng intoned. "Silence, the slaves are coming. Audacity, more audacity, endless audacity."

"Yes, yes. Ha ha ha!" cried Nora at the top of her lungs, but when she saw the girl coming back with one of the other women who worked in the kitchen, she started muttering quietly and so quickly that it was almost another language. The tourists came to their windows and out onto their porches. A few of the children sidled closer.

"Sometimes it calms her down to eat something," said the woman, who'd been at the hotel longer than the girl. "Go get the sancocho. I'll keep her entertained. Give her a big helping – she sure does eat! Don't bring a knife or fork, just one of those plastic spoons."

"She can't even keep her cunt entertained and now she wants to entertain you," the wicked Carlota, of the many facelifts, of the face plastered with nauseating makeup, whispered in her ear, and she let herself be provoked:

"You can't even keep your cunt entertained and now you want to entertain me," she repeated too loudly, and the scandalized mothers who were watching it all from their porches with their children would no doubt complain to the King afterward, if he ever returned.

"And tell her she can stick that plastic spoon up her ass," Carlota added, and Nora couldn't help repeating it.

When the sancocho arrived, there were no longer any children on the porches or anywhere else, except the ones who'd hidden to watch from behind the coconut palms and almond trees. The mothers had also gone inside, exclaiming, "Unbeliev-able, saying such vile things in front of innocent children! Holy Jesus, Mary, and Joseph!" Other mothers had said to forgive her for she knew not what she said, but they, too, had gone into their bungalows with their offspring.

The sancocho calmed Nora's agitated spirits. Alarmed by her lack of prudence, more prudence, endless prudence, which might lead to devastating consequences, she wordlessly, using her humiliating plastic spoon, tucked into the delectable potatoes, yams, and chunks of sea bass. "Spectacular, spectac-ular," she said. Up in the ceiling, the rabbit winked at her and wiggled its ears. For a few seconds, Nora stopped eating. Brains. Starting today, her strategy would be to retreat while moving forward, like in tai chi. The sancocho disappeared quickly, but her hunger increased.

"She wants seconds!" intoned the throng. "Queen Sahamarakahanda V wants seconds!"

"Who?" asked the new girl, and the other woman explained:

"It's her. It doesn't matter. Don't pay it any mind. Let her have seconds if she wants. Go get her another helping. That way she'll fall asleep faster and let us sleep."

"Why don't they just put her in the loony bin?" asked a harpy from within one of the guest bungalows.

She must have been one of wicked Carlota's allies. Nora was about to insult her in that unique way of hers, but the girl had reappeared with the sancocho, so she had more urgent matters to attend to.

"Endless guile," said Nora with her mouth full, pointing a wise, admonishing index finger at the new girl.

"What's that?"

"You're from Sahagún."

"How did you know, ma'am?"

"You see. I know everything that happens on these beaches. And you're also very pretty."

"Thank you, ma'am."

"You can go."

The girl from Sahagún would be saved from the bloodbath and was thenceforth pardoned. After her second helping, Nora began to feel tired from all the tubers, however delicious they'd been, and though she'd have liked to eat more, her growing lack of appetite made that impossible. She got up from the table, went out onto the porch again, and walked, clad in her slip, among the palm trees illuminated by the light from the bungalows. Reaching the shore, she sat down in a plastic chair there in the darkness, far from the light of the lampposts, which mercilessly flooded the wide strip of sand in front of the hotel. The sancocho had satiated her, but she didn't want to go to bed again without seeing the stars, before the wind wiped them out and the world came to an end.

She also wanted to see the sea foam, which was beautiful even though her two sons were tangled up in it, each wearing a crown of thorns, as if they were in a burning bush. The girl from Sahagún watched her from a distance, certain that Nora hadn't seen her.

Nora was about to summon her magnanimously to her side and ask her to accompany her in gazing at what might well be the last night of the universe, but she changed her mind, thinking that the girl might be a neatly packaged hypocrite hired by her husband and the lackey government to spy on her. She didn't believe it, but it was always best to be mindful in this world, where everything always ended up disappearing or turning into pain. Prudence.

Then, out of nowhere, the children appeared in the distance, a herd of them hollering in the night. They ran past her without seeing her, wielding flashlights and sticks to chase and destroy crabs in the starlight.

9:00 p.m.

After Javier told him to shut up, damn it, the father had fallen silent. Almost an hour later, he still remained silent. The school of tarpon had left, and fish were scarce. Javier broke his promise not to smoke marijuana during the fishing expedition and groped around in his bag for the jar. He also pulled out one of those headlamps like miners use and turned it on so he could fill his pipe. The father didn't say anything, either about the light or the marijuana. Mario didn't object to the light either, though it would scare off the fish even more. Javier took three long tokes on the pipe, put it away again, and felt at peace. Without removing the lamp from his head, he turned it off so he could see the black sea that surrounded them and look up at the flashes of the distant storm. The water Mario disturbed as he fished sounded like music.

"Yeah?" Javier asked.

"Snapper. Medium size."

He could barely see Mario and his father. They'd both crossed to the other side, belonged to chaos rather than to light, were specters rather than living beings. Javier took three deep breaths, something he always did whenever marijuana suddenly threatened to open the doors of darkness and horror. If his father had said anything right then, if he'd hurled some barb or bit of sarcasm, Javier would have plunged irretrievably into hell, but the father didn't say anything. With momentous effort, Javier was therefore able to return to this world of ours, where things are what they seem – a rose is a rose and a storm is just a storm –

and he watched the silent glow of the here-and-now storm with deep admiration. The bolts of lightning overlapped and varied in intensity and duration, as if expressing an extraordinary and inhuman emotion.

"I smoked too much. I can't pass out now," he thought, and had to work hard to keep his father's silence in the darkness from overpowering him.

"Pass me a thermos," he said to Mario.

His brother moved comfortably in the darkness. Javier heard him pour coffee into the lid of the thermos, which they used as a cup, and move toward him.

"Here," said Mario, and handed him the cup.

With the coffee, Javier regained a degree of equanimity, though he was still catching glimpses, like little flashes, of the monstrousness of life. He took three more deep breaths and managed to calm down. Tranquility restored, he decided to stop fishing for a while. He reeled in his lines, as if he were going to switch the bait, and cast them again, empty, into the sea. He looked up at the sky, hoping to see a shooting star, and felt content even though he didn't see one.

It occurred to him that if all it took was three deep puffs of *Cannabis sativa* to provoke such distress, poor Sahamaraka-handa's world must be unbearable. Sometimes Javier would look at her or listen to her and wonder if she ever experienced moments of happiness, or if instead she lived in an endless, stupefying inferno. *You could wonder the same thing about people who are sane*, he thought. In the books he'd read so far, people were almost never happy. In Shakespeare's plays, which he read as if they were novels, but whose immense power overwhelmed him, the closest thing to happiness was found in the fleeting frenzy of greed or triumphant revenge, before the characters' ultimate undoing. Javier had read somewhere that a person is born not to be happy but to admire the world. When joy comes, it does so without rhyme or reason, just because. *I mean, take me, living it up out here with sore butt cheeks at nine thirty at night, on a boat with two men who want to claw each other's eyes out.*

He rummaged for his cigarettes and lighter in his bag, and the smoke dissipated invisibly into the night. He found beauty in the ember of the cigarette, which looked to his father and brother as if it were suspended in the air, like a firefly. The light from a star, the cherry of the Pielroja cigarette, and the light of a firefly were all exactly the same. None of the three mattered. People didn't matter either. His father was a miserable loser who was convinced he was a king. Sahamarakahando V. And now the King's ankle was all fucked up and his soul was a pit of bile. And he himself wasn't anything either, thought Javier. And that was actually the beauty of it all.

He turned on the headlamp again and pulled a beer out of the basket. There were some cold ones in the cooler next to his father, but getting to them would be complicated. The bottle opener was in the cooler too, so he uncapped the beer by striking it against the side of the boat. The sound boomed in the oceanic night. Javier switched off the headlamp and sipped his beer slowly to avoid the unpleasant sensation of the lukewarm carbonation tickling his tongue and foaming too much in his throat. Astutely, the father realized his son didn't want to come near him. *The guy in that story who gets walled in suddenly goes quiet, just like him, when he realizes he's being walled in*, thinks Javier, who is once more invaded by dark thoughts and focuses instead on the tapestry of stars and the gentle euphoria produced by the beer. He switches on the headlamp and checks his watch. Nine forty. The father hasn't said a word for more than fifty minutes. Javier nearly asks how his ankle's doing, but in the end he doesn't say anything. *I don't give a crap how his ankle's doing*, he thinks.

"What's up with you and that headlamp?" asks Mario, and Javier turns it off.

Again they hear the sound of a fish being heaved into the boat, and Javier feels an involuntary twinge of admiration for his father, who, despite everything, has kept fishing in silence. Listening to the club strike the fish, Javier thinks how God does shoddy work. *We Playamar monkeys enjoy butchering pigs, wringing chickens' necks, and clubbing fish. And then chewing them up and swallowing.* Like Mario, Javier is constantly aware of the cruelty of Creation, though his awareness is much less intense and naïve than his brother's. His amazement at the slaughterhouse of life springs less from a sense of pity for animals than from an aesthetic one – *It is what it is, and who the hell gives a shit about a chicken?* Plus, if God was so slapdash when it came to justice, that means, doesn't it, that when it comes down to it, they could do whatever they want. Which they never did, of course, at least not in serious instances. But a man decides to respect others only of his own free will, Javier thinks, and he can decide otherwise just as freely.

Javier contemplated how his thoughts were pushing insistently into labyrinths where the world no longer had an up or a down and murder became conceivable. The sounds coming from the father's side weighed on him more and more, and he pricked up his ears and attempted to decipher them: a fish had just nibbled on his father's line, he'd just changed the bait on one of his lines, the bait had been stolen from another, maybe he'd leaned against the side of the boat to urinate . . . There were some noises that Javier didn't recognize immediately – the sound of a foot being inserted again into the cooler full of ice and fish, the gurgling of the water in the jug as the father drank – and there were murmurs that were almost clear though not unambiguous, like when the father seemed to say "Damn ankle" or maybe "If it weren't for this damned ankle," and ones where Javier couldn't be sure whether he was hearing them because his father was thinking them, or if he was really hearing them out loud. And all of the sounds commingled with the lapping of the water against the hull and became indeterminate and infinite.

Then he heard, this time unmistakably, the father's voice, speaking as if he'd finally risen from the dead:

"Gotcha!"

The father switched on his flashlight and, still seated, began fighting with what would turn out to be one of the largest groupers Javier had ever seen. Four hundred pounds, if not more. But they didn't end up getting that fish into the bottom of the boat either. Though the twins both offered to take care of the animal, the father refused to hand over his rod or even respond to their offers. Sitting on his bench, huffing and cursing, he struggled with the fish for a long time and finally lost it when it was right next to the boat, as if the fish had halted its approach of its own accord to make sure they would shine their lights on it and see it in the full glory of its tremendous size and power. Then it broke the fishing line and vanished, victorious, into the vastness of the dark water that was striking the sides of the boat with increasing intensity.

"The old bastard pulled till the line just snapped," said Mario, not nearly under his breath, after turning off his flashlight.

10:00 p.m.
I had a hard time sleeping that night. I wasn't used to sleeping in a hammock or having so many people under a single roof. I'm the tourist who came to go camping on the islands with my wife and son. I had a powerful itch to scratch! My wife and I had been arguing that evening – she says I become insufferable when plans change – and I didn't like the idea of leaving our tent on the beach because of the storm. She never would have welcomed me into her hammock under those circumstances, and even if I'd managed to convince her, I haven't mastered the art of making love in midair, and the dirt floor wasn't a viable option. In an effort to distract myself, I listened to the thunderclaps booming in the distance, one after and on top of the other, and smoked. When I left the house, I didn't even look at the people sleeping in hammocks and on canvas cots in the other rooms, like in a

refugee camp. Using the flashlight, I followed the path through the mangroves to the beach where we'd been camping, to not just see but bear witness to the lightning and the stars, which, despite being opposites, seemed to have spilled simultaneously across the heavenly vault. It sure does make a man feel tiny, with his watercolors and charcoals, to stand face to face with something like that! Only the greats, like Turner, dare paint the totality; the rest of us can, at most, strive to capture parts, details, with the hope and aim that they will evoke the whole. And so, sitting on the sand, I lost myself in these disquisitions, attempting to ward off the erotic images harassing me from all sides.

No boat lights were glowing out at sea. The fishing boats from the industrial fleet based in Tolú had been berthed at the docks to shelter them from mishap if the tempest ended up visiting us here in the gulf. And later the harbor master had forbidden the smaller boats from going out, especially those used by the local independent fishermen. I'd learned all of that from Javier, the young man from the Playamar bungalows who's become a friend, the bookish one we ran into at the island's general store when he came in to buy beer.

"Most likely the sea's going to be really rough tonight," he said.

"But you're going out anyway?" I asked.

His reply was brief and had a brusque Antioquian tinge to it, though it was uttered in a coastal accent: "We've got to die of something, right? Nobody lives forever. Plus, who's going to convince the old bastard to stand down?"

I asked what he was reading, and we started talking about *Macbeth*, of all things. In the hot, jumbled store – at that time of day, the Milo chocolate powder had practically turned to liquid in its tins – Javier, all tanned and barefoot and shirtless, wearing yellow shorts and a Yankees cap, spoke rapidly and fervently about the scene where Lady Macbeth washes the blood from her hands. We drank a couple of ice-cold beers. We also discussed *King Lear*, and he got so worked up that, after a few impassioned observations ("The old man really outdid himself in the dipshit department, didn't he?"), he fell silent, seemingly still pondering the subject. Or maybe he remembered they were waiting on him, so he gulped down the second beer in a hurry. Javier didn't put on intellectual airs; he was simply astonished by what the king had allowed to happen to him. "All right, man, we'll talk soon, David, see you around. Good luck," he said. I invited him to have another beer, but he said no, no can do. He had to go; his old man was probably going to have a fit, he'd taken so long.

So, as I was saying, I'd been feeling suffocated in that crowded house and decided to go down to the beach for a smoke.

With my wife relatively far away and my erection under control, I serenely contemplated the sea. Above it, the blackness of the storm had begun to advance, blotting out the stars. Somewhere out there, the three of them were in their boat, watching, like me, as the sky grew smudged and the water choppy. With the gale blowing on the back of his neck, Javier would be thinking about the tragedies he'd been reading, where all the characters, from beginning to end, had death blowing on the backs of their necks. In my mind, images of the three fishermen with the storm looming over them like a grim angel came one after another, distinctive in their lack of edges, in the way they were already half immersed in chaos, paintings that strove to portray the oily affections and animosities of those three precarious beings on the verge of falling apart.

We are the tourists.

I'm Yónatan again, grandson of Doña Libe, the woman from the bungalows down the way. I'm eight years old and look like I'm seven, but I'm really smart even though I'm little, and when I came back from killing crabs, I was starving. My grandmother was waiting for me on the beach. "Heavens, Yónatan, it's getting late!" she said. "Don't you realize the storm that's coming in? If it catches you fooling around on the beach with those other goof-off kids, one of those waves'll get you and you won't even have time for an aspiration." An aspiration is something like *All glory be to God*. So you're walking along the beach minding your own business and you barely manage to squeak out, "All glory be . . ." before, boom, the wave's got you. My grandma says I'm a real card. The other boys and I were planning to sneak out at around ten that night, as soon as the storm started, to go watch it and see the waves they say are as big as two-story houses. Sneak out? What a joke! When I woke up, it was already the next day, and I looked out the window and the beach was full of trash and branches. Everybody said they'd never seen such a big one, and there were even toys buried in the sand. Still wearing my PJs, I went over to the manager's house, and her kids and I started looking at all the things the water had brought. I found a beat-up, faded Darth Vader helmet, and my grandma told me I looked like a mushroom wearing it.

And I'm Johanna, the one whose boyfriend stayed out in the sun too long the first day and got burned to a crisp – that was so careless, going swimming without a T-shirt or sunblock even though he's so pale. So I didn't hear much about them, the three fishermen, because I was worried about my boyfriend's fever – he started raving and insisting we couldn't let him die. "Nobody dies of sunburn, silly," I told him, but he was still scared, saying he'd dreamed about some old sows that were going to carry him off to God knows where. I'm sure he was freaked out because of the owner's crazy wife, who suddenly started shouting in the middle of the night about some lady named Carlota and calling her a horrible old sow. I went to the office to complain and see if they could recommend a doctor for Ricardo, but . . . office? What a joke! The so-called office is the owner's house, and of course he was one of the fishermen who was out at sea, the moron, and with his sons too. Everybody was saying they were going to drown.

The cook came – she'd spent the night in a hammock in the kitchen so she could look after the crazy lady, who'd been agitated that day. She told me the nearest doctor was in Tolú, but that there was no need to call him over a sunburn. Between the two of us, we got poor Ricardo up and into some cool water to get his fever down. He was so disoriented that he barely complained about us hurting him when we helped him into the shower. We gave him two extra-strength aspirin. Just what the doctor ordered! He went to sleep and slept so deeply I actually started worrying – it seemed like he was in a coma, or worse. And later the wind came and lightning loud enough to raise the dead, and the waves booming like they were right outside our door. The seawater was rushing between the guest bungalows, and he didn't even notice. The water even came into ours, but only a little, since they were elevated on concrete slabs, but I sometimes felt like more was going to come flooding in and snatch us away. I swept the water out with the broom, and when I thought it had seeped back in, I'd relight the candle – the power had gone out – and get up to push the sea away again with the broom.

11:00 p.m.
It's going to take a lot more than a couple of losers and some fucking waves to get rid of me, the father thinks to himself. His ankle hurts a lot, but he's tired of propping his foot up for relief on the cooler that now contains fish, cold water, and very little ice, and he's braced to just suffer through the pain, as if he'd been born with it. From time to time, using the oar as a crutch, he gets to his feet – not to do anything, since he's doing everything sitting down, but to make sure he's not completely incapacitated and at his sons' mercy.

The fish start biting like crazy again.

Father and sons hook sea bass and blue runners and goatfish and tuna, and they've barely baited and cast their lines when they have to reel them in again. The boat floor, where only large fish remain – the rest of them, neatly gutted, are in the coolers – becomes covered with medium-size fish that gape and flop in the darkening night. The father estimates they've got about six hundred pounds and they need to bring in nine hundred, including their catch so far. There are no more stars in the sky, and the darkness is so deep they can't even see one another. The father first smells pot, then a Pielroja cigarette. He's never smoked and can't stand addictions. He considers his fondness for alcohol to be not a weakness but a professional tool, since he's chatty when he drinks and quiet when he doesn't – hospitality is an effort for him.

He shivers in the chilly air. The waves are lifting the boat higher and higher, and the lightning is growing closer and louder. When Javier tells him that if they leave "right this minute" they'll elude the storm and make it back to the hotel beach, the father makes a decision once and for all: betting the storm won't catch them head on, they'll keep fishing till they hit the quota he's set. It'll be less than two hours, he guesses, and it's not for sure that the storm's going to come this way in the first place. Plus, even if there'd been a chance he'd agree to flee the storm like a bunch of chickens, Javier's imperious "right this minute" would have made it impossible. *Right this minute? I'll show you right this minute, asshole*, the father thinks viciously.

"Right this minute?" he asks aloud, like an echo, nearly choking. More than anything, in his rage, he'd like to seem scathing, but there are so many things he wants to say, he can't get them out.

"Goddammit, it's going to take a lot more than a couple of pussies still living at home to make me turn tail before I've run into so much as a little ocean spray. Your mother spoiled you two rotten, if you ask me. Leave now, when the fish are practically flinging themselves into the boat? I'm no idiot!" The father always has something to say about the twins. He can't really deem them cowards, since it's clear Mario wouldn't mind ending up floating facedown in the sea amid the storm debris, and Javier's fully justified unease is nowhere near turning into panic. But judging his sons harshly has become a habit by now, almost a hobby, regardless of the truth of things. As he sees it, the fact that they haven't struck out on their own by now, at twenty-six, gives him the right to say anything he wants.

Javier doesn't respond. Calming down, the father focuses on his fishing rods; he's so sure of himself, he forgets about the oncoming storm and especially about his sons' feelings, which are as palpable as gusts of wind. His ankle throbs. Javier's headlamp goes on as the twin replaces the hook a fish has just carried off. The father studies his son's profile without affection. The waves are getting higher, but they're moving slowly, so the swell isn't making them seasick. The father has been hauling fish in literally right and left – a lot more than his sons have, he thinks. Afraid they're all going to end up at the bottom of the sea, the twins are working listlessly – they're young and lazy, no drive, no conviction. *And look at them smoking again*, he thinks when he sees the smoke dimming the glow of Javier's headlamp.

"The light," says Mario. A few seconds go by, and Javier doesn't turn off his lamp. "The light, asshole. You're a real pain in the ass, huh?"

The father shakes with mounting fever. Before the lamp goes out, he catches a glimpse of the masses of water now swelling and sinking beneath the boat. Perhaps in the grip of fever, he surveys them with both admiration and scorn. On the afternoons he spends drinking aguardiente at Playamar, the father always tells his guests he has a lot of respect for the sea – but he says it not to describe a real feeling but because it sounds good and is the sort of cliché that tourists who come down to the coast from Antioquia like to hear and carry away with them afterward as a souvenir, like a piece of local handicraft, back to the mountains, where they repeat it to impress those who have never seen the sea. Before buying the hectare and a half of land to build the hotel, the father analyzed the tourist industry for several months. Baffled though he was by Medellín residents' penchant for frying in the sun on the scorching sand, that was none of his concern. That impulse – it was crystal-clear from the beginning – was as powerful and ineluctable as sea turtles' egg-laying ritual and therefore enormously profitable for vacation-bungalow owners. There was nothing to stop him from getting in on the score. So he surveyed the palm trees, the wide stretch of beach, confirmed that the subsoil contained sufficient and easily accessible freshwater, calculated how many units he'd be able to build in an initial phase, did some sums, paid for the land, and started building the first three bungalows, which soon paid for themselves and funded the construction of another seven. Though Nora and the boys were with him and she hadn't gotten sick yet, the father never took her needs into consideration; he did everything as if he were on his own.

Of course he enjoyed the color of the sea, the whiteness of the beaches, the gannets flying overhead, but he so often heard from guests how beautiful the place was and how it was worth preserving that in time their praise began to irritate him, as if he were being forced to listen to two people making love. And though he wouldn't have thought twice about selling the hotel to anyone who agreed to his asking price, he was truly attached to the place and even somewhat fond of it. To give it an eco-friendly vibe, which is always good for business, he attached green plastic trash cans to the trunks of the palm trees and put up signs in the showers that said, "Water belongs to all of us. Conserve it." But he was a realist and saved on the cost of a new septic tank by directing wastewater from the two rearmost bungalows through pipes that dumped straight into the mangrove swamp. You could smell it in those bungalows, and only in them, but very few guests complained. Most of them figured that was the way the air sometimes smelled at the seaside.

A bolt of lightning strikes not far from the boat, and the glow turns it to mercury. The father is blinded and dazed. He is bristling with fever in the deep darkness that follows lightning, and his teeth are chattering again.

"Don't give me that shit right now," he tells the lightning or whoever's responsible for it. "A couple of big booms aren't going to scare me – I'm a man, not a goddamn pussy."

Aloft on a wave in total darkness, along with his boat and his two sons, the father starts reeling in one of his lines. A powerful fish, maybe a barracuda – though its tugging feels strange, like that of a human or another intelligent creature – puts up such a fight that the father doesn't even notice how the boat is rising higher toward the blackness above and sinking farther toward the ocean depths. The storm may have failed to frighten him, but fear now rises in his throat because of the fish he's hooked. Lightning bolts of pain shoot through his ankle, and he ignores them just as he does the lightning that's crackling nearby and illuminating the boat as it scales the mountains of water. He is overwhelmed and worried by the creature he is fighting to pull out of the sea, but he keeps reeling in his line, tempted though he is to let go of the rod and allow it to plunge with the fish, just like that, into the abyss. Pride and fury stiffen his resolve. All at once the fish stops pulling, and it's as if the line has broken or as if the father never caught anything in the first place. And when he starts to reel it in, the crushing weight returns and he has to cling to the rod with all his might so the sudden tug doesn't pull it from his grasp. Part of him thinks it's another huge grouper.

There are things the father doesn't hear. He doesn't hear Mario when he asks Javier what's going on over there with the old bastard, and he doesn't hear Javier when he says he chose a bad time to get hurt. He doesn't hear Javier when he tells Mario that he, the father, probably has a broken ankle, or hear Mario reply that he hopes it gets infected, that'll teach him a lesson. It's possible that at times the twins can't even hear each other, since the thunder has become a constant growl even though it's not on top of them yet and the wind hasn't yet started to blow or the rain to fall. And most of all the father doesn't hear Javier when he says they should head back to shore.

Suddenly he's alone. The pain in his ankle becomes as external as the thunder and lightning, and his sons disappear. Rising from the abyss toward the surface, toward them, comes an unknown *something* that provokes horror in the father, and tries to get into the boat. It's not a fish. He's delirious. Everything around him merges with the tall waves, and he forgets that they're only fifty feet above the coral reefs and not suspended above an abyss. "You're not going to bring me down, you bastards," he says, attempting to sound resolute.

But he's afraid. He's hardly ever been afraid in his life.

Sunday, 12:01 a.m.
Mario heard his father talking to himself in the darkness in a feverish voice, a madman's voice, and felt uneasy. Now what? His brother turned on his headlamp, and Mario saw his father hurriedly cut one of the lines, retreat in terror, and tumble into the water. Javier leaped up, grabbed the father by the arms, and hauled him back into the boat, which was now atop an immense wave.

"Let's go, let's go," said Javier, and Mario started the motor, which sounded flimsy, almost nonexistent, in the rolling thunder.

It was about two hours from where they were to the hotel beach in normal conditions. Now there was no way of knowing how long it would be. One and a half, if the waves were in their favor; four, if the winds picked up or the sea was against them; an eternity, easily, if the storm came down on them with all its fury. In any case they'd have to avoid sailing through the islands and go around them, approaching the gulf via deeper waters. Mario felt an exultation akin to happiness, not so much because of the father's apparent defeat, which under the current circumstances he didn't really have time to consider and appreciate, but because he felt that he had the world at his command through the Evinrude's steering arm. Mario watched as Javier, without consulting anybody, tossed the coolers holding their catch overboard, and then the large fish in the bottom of the boat. He saw him sit down and shine a light on the father, who was raving in the bow, clutching his head in his hands – hoarse with terror because of what he claimed he'd been about to pull out of the water – and keep shining it on him, as if he was afraid that at any moment the older man might leap into the sea. *Just look at him playing the good son now, the twerp,* Mario thought.

The boat, illuminated by his and Javier's flashlights and by the intermittent lightning, moved through the masses of water as they rose in search of the highest blackness and then sank again, drawn by the bottom of the sea. Mario had an instinct for catching the waves in the darkness, and he knew he was a better boatman than his father, even if nobody acknowledged it. For as long as he could remember, he'd been floating in the sea: on tree trunks when he was practically a baby, and later on rafts that he and the other kids built, which they impelled along the sandy bottom using mangrove poles; on rafts with crude sails, in skiffs, in sloops, and in motorized sailboats. But when he went out with his father, he sometimes felt inhibited by his father's presence and would end up making mistakes, big mistakes, ones that would have been inconceivable in other circumstances.

"Old bastard," he'd mutter then.

Old bastard, he thought now. The waves were as tall as houses, but as wide as rice paddies or baseball fields, and gentle in that vastness. And though he didn't say anything, Mario thought his brother had been wrong to throw out the fish. They'd sailed rougher seas than these, and while the storm might grow stronger, it also might not. *Sometimes weed makes problems seem bigger than they are – your perception gets out of whack*, he thought. *That's at least six hundred pounds down the tubes.*

Mario also didn't agree with the decision to turn back. The only reason he hadn't objected was that he enjoyed navigating the choppy seas, but he would rather have stayed where they were until the storm passed, since if it had hit them, it wouldn't have been with much force. As the boat perched briefly at the crest of a wave, Mario thought he saw the lights of one of the islands in front of them. No point in asking Javier. The father, with his keen eyesight, could have confirmed it, but look at him there, totally useless. Despite his euphoria, Mario couldn't help feeling astonished by the state his father was in. He and Javier had never seen him laid out like that, not even on those rare occasions when he'd had too much to drink or come down with the flu. Seeing him now, Mario felt a mix of revulsion, fear, and indifference, similar to what one might feel at watching the death throes of a rabid dog. The boat climbed once more to the summit of a wave, and this time he had no doubt he was seeing the lights from the nearest island, the one where they'd bought the beer. He shouted to his brother.

"Yeah, we'd better get clear," Javier replied.

Mario turned the boat to start moving away from the islands toward the center of the gulf. He thought he'd heard the waves crashing against the nearby reefs. The islands themselves were probably being walloped by the surf, and any tourists camping in tents would already have been flooded out. *Back at Playamar, the sea will be rushing through the mangrove swamp, like it always does*, he thought. *The nutcase must be freaking out with all the thunder.* He had to meet the waves practically head on to get the boat out into open water where there was no risk that the crushing billows would sink them. It was slow going, since they were moving against the swell, but once they were in deeper waters, Mario turned again and headed toward the middle of the gulf, moving in the same direction as the waves but taking them on the diagonal so they didn't carry the boat ashore. The father had curled up on the floor between two benches, or maybe Javier had laid him there, and he looked like he was sleeping, using the bag as a pillow and with water lapping against part of his shoulder, arm, and leg. Javier was bailing with a coconut bowl. In the glow of the lightning, Mario could see that the storm was giving signs of changing directions. If the old man hadn't looked so rough, they could have gone back and started fishing. Javier had really pulled a dumb move, dumping everything overboard.

There was no strong wind, no rain, and the waves were becoming smaller and less frequent. In the bottom of the boat, the father looked like he was dead. *He was acting weird even before he fucked up his ankle,* Mario thought.

"I don't think it's a stroke," said Javier, as if reading his thoughts. "He does have a really high fever. We need to get back and take him straight to Montería. Whatever's going on, it's serious."

He says "get back" like we're just out running errands or something. If this tub capsizes, nobody's getting anywhere. We have to get within reach, so to speak, but nobody's going to try to make land with the waves crashing at Playamar. If he had a stroke, too bad. There's nothing we can do, even if we end up with a swimming pool in here, thought Mario without conviction, since he knew he was capable of getting the boat to shore safe and sound with all of its occupants, no matter the conditions. The gulf's beaches were wide and clear, no rocks or boulders, pure sand, so you just had to know how to work the waves.

The boat kept moving swiftly through extreme darkness that alternated with the extreme brightness of the lightning. The bow struck the large waves, shattered them, and the water surged over the twins. In the fiberglass microcosm of the boat, which had gone from sky-blue to now black, Mario saw Javier shine his tiny headlamp on their father, adjust the injured man's head on the bag so he wouldn't choke on the water that had accumulated in the bottom of the boat, and start bailing again.

1:00 a.m.
When Nora opened her eyes, the lightning demons made of ice and coal were flying everywhere, and the chorus's chanting boomed out between the thunderclaps. The marsupial-snouted

donkey was waiting. The explosions of the sea were crashing down on the beach.

"The instrument of my redemption."

"With Imogenia destroyed, foul-smelling Carlota will be forever silent, and your sons will be saved from the surging waters," the throng prophesied.

The cook would have to die. The chorus had been showing Nora the way, which was both tricky and simple: she would have to come up with some pretext to summon the woman to her bungalow, and as soon as the cook entered the bedroom, the weight of universal justice would come down on her skull.

"Her filthy spirit will then travel on ragged wings to Hades, flying through bats and palm fronds," the chorus sang. "Harbor no compassion. Did he harbor it for you or your sons, who are threatening at this very moment to annihilate him and annihilate themselves? Remember, Sahamarakahanda, he had no qualms about bringing the young concubine and his son here and smearing them on your face like chicken feces."

"Like feces. Exactly," Nora nodded, pensive, sad, practically sobbing with fury.

The throng went quiet to make space for whatever would happen next, and once their clamor had ended, the thunder and the booming of the sea retook center stage. Nora cried out in the night split by lightning. The cook might or might not come. Nobody knew. Nora picked up a chair and started breaking everything she could. Then the hammer-eared donkey came down from the ceiling and Nora, certain that her plan would triumph, stood next to the door and kept shouting. The sea descended toward the mangrove swamp. The wind roared across the rooftops and through the palm trees, but not enough to bend them or quiet Nora's cries, so it was no surprise to anybody that Imogenia had tried to turn on the light in the kitchen and, upon discovering the power had gone out, as it often did during storms, then switched on her flashlight and, pushed along by the powerful wind, headed to Nora's bungalow.

"Shattering of glasses. Blood," cried two of the prophets. "If you fail, coral will gouge out the boys' eyes."

Nora's shouting grew louder and louder, but the cook was taking a long time to arrive, so Nora and the others figured she'd decided to go for help before coming to the bungalow. The donkey would have to take a break and make sure the cook was the first one to enter the room so that she, and only she, could fulfill her destiny. There was a knock at the bungalow door.

Then Carlota intervened.

Carlota was an ant, a cockroach, a green bottle poop fly that had been trapped in the bungalow and buzzed swiftly in Nora's ear to distract her. The cook had come on her own after all – she'd walked to the bedroom door and unhesitatingly opened it, but with Nora distracted, the startled rabbit tore the air asunder and everything turned to smoke, turned to nothing, turned to emptiness. When she came back from the air, Nora found herself on the bed, trussed up like a baby goat. Many faces were smothering her breath. There were normal ones and monstrous ones. Some with chicken beaks and some that were beautiful and serene in their wickedness. And all of them wanted to destroy her, and they cursed her and insulted her so she'd abandon wisdom and become lost. The existence of the universe and her own now depended on her ability to remain still. To steel herself, she thought, *Star silence of my sons, silence mine, boat silence, house silence, high sea, seventh that terrifies, jealousy mine, my life no longer calls out. If death takes place in the heavens, everything will slough away if the sky turns green after death. The cheerful fountainhead endures. Endless fatigue. Fragile are those who have never loved. Silence. Silence . . .*

"Loosen the ties a little. Her hands are turning purple."

"She was fighting so hard, she actually cut herself. She's dying, Imogenia. Her eyes are rolled back."

"What would she be dying of? Don't be an idiot! Nobody hit her, nobody did anything to her. It's a miracle she didn't take my head off."

"She's gotten so fat – a heart attack or something. She looked like she was possessed, the way she was punching and screaming at Carlota, didn't she, Imo? And she's so heavy, just impossible to handle. She sure does eat! Even with four of us, she was still kicking."

"Uh-huh. And who's this Carlota woman? She talks about her all the time, as if she came by every day."

"You tell me."

"At least she'll be calm when they come back, the old man and the boys."

"Yeah."

"If they come back."

"Yeah."

"They're so reckless."

"The seas are quieting down. The storm wasn't so bad."

"Not here. It did a lot of damage around Rincón. The radio said so. I'm worried about my family up there, Imogenia."

"Is she asleep?"

"Her eyes are closed."

Candle that I gave him. Knot in his throat the night I saw him. And now I am all alone, far from my sons, far from everything! All I have is that image that agitates me, only that figure that takes my breath away and which I'd rather not name . . .

"Have they come back?" Nora asked.

"No," said Imogenia.

"Did they drown?"

"Who?" asked the husband.

"What do you mean *who*, dummy? No, Doña Nora, they'll be back soon."

My mouth, fishing line that embraces him, thought Nora. Thread of blood in my mouth. Family tombstone. Barrier and hay. Barrier and sweet. Barrier and prostration.

"No, don't just loosen the cords," said Imogenia. "She's calm. Untie her right now."

2:00 a.m.

Javier saw the wave racing toward the bow, lit by a flash of lightning, and managed to grab one of the ropes they'd used to lash the oars to the hull and ride out the pounding, inhuman pull of the sea, which seemed to invade his lungs.

Up until that point, they'd been sailing well, since the wind wasn't at full force and the waves, though they reached towering heights, were not crashing down. In the glow of the lightning, they looked like huge mountains gently collapsing – impressive, yes, but almost benevolent in their power – and nothing had presaged the one that came toward them against the tide, crashed over them, raked the boat, and carried off everything in it except the gas cans, the anchor, the motor, and the twins. The oars, the pole, the hook, the bucket of bait, the bags, the jugs of water, the basket of beer, the fishing rods, and the buckets of reels were all swept overboard. The father was snatched by the sea.

Javier coughed, took a deep breath, and coughed and inhaled again until he was able to catch his breath. He felt the water lapping above his ankles and realized he needed to start bailing immediately. He called out to Mario and Mario responded; he called to his father and silence replied. Thunder boomed. The Evinrude started up again, and Javier saw Mario's flashlight go on and sweep over the entire boat, especially the place where their father had been, and then go off again. He heard the motor rev and keep sailing in the same direction as before, as if they hadn't just been hit by a wave and been on the point of shipwreck. As if they hadn't lost everything and their father hadn't been snatched by the sea.

In his astonishment, it took Javier, holding the bailing bowl, a moment to react.

"What the hell are you doing? Shit!" he shouted. "Hey, hey! Turn around! Turn around, damn it!"

His brother seemed to have gone deaf.

They couldn't hear their father shouting from the darkness of the water, and when the lightning flashed, they couldn't see him floating or waving his arms or swimming anywhere. Javier kept yelling at Mario to turn back, but his brother didn't answer. Javier sat there a moment, in silence, and felt dizzy. The boat was moving inexorably away from where the father had fallen overboard. Javier went over to his brother and, without yelling at him, without saying a word, punched him in the face and then the head with all his might, his knuckles almost shattering, trying to stun his brother and seize control of the boat, which started to yaw so that at any moment they might be struck by a wave from the side and shipwreck for real this time.

Mario, only half conscious, crashed to the bottom of the boat. Javier grabbed the flashlight, took over the steering arm, and, in a daze and distressed by his brother's inert body, didn't make sure to take the wave on the diagonal as he changed course, and they nearly capsized. He managed to get the boat upright again and started shouting, illuminating the mountains of water with the tiny flashlight. He was relieved to see his brother sit up and start to bail, but since Mario still looked pretty out of it, he didn't ask him to yell too, and instead kept shouting on his own.

Javier was right not to expect much from Mario when it came to rescuing their father, since the first thing he said once he'd pulled himself back together was:

"The old bastard drowned. Let's go."

"Keep bailing, keep bailing or we'll sink."

Javier continued shouting till his throat began to hurt. The beam of light flitted to and fro, almost comically minuscule in the vast darkness, and the boat moved in aimless circles through the massive waves. "We're nothing, we're worth absolutely nothing," Javier used to say on those late nights when he'd had a lot to drink or smoke and his mood grew dark. Now the infinite world of darkness proved him right. There was nothing left of the father. He'd disappeared into the sea like a drop of ink or oil.

"Take the steering arm and keep going in circles," Javier ordered, and Mario didn't dare disobey. *I can go around in circles all night, but that's not going to make the old bastard rise up from the sea floor and crash back onto his seat*, his body language seemed to say when Javier sternly pointed the flashlight at him. The minutes stretched out so long that to Javier it seemed as if the world had become a bell of anxiety, without a before or an after. He was terrified that he and Mario, especially Mario, might have to bear the burden of their dead father for the rest of their lives. He shouted for his father, illuminating the waves and bailing at the same time, and after a while he was ready to jump into the sea himself. He shouted at his brother to call out, but Mario didn't, though he kept tracing large circles with the boat in the darkness. They'd taken on a lot of water. He ordered Mario to leave the motor in neutral and start bailing, and when the twin obeyed, they heard their father's voice, very weak, as if it were coming from the air and not the sea.

Time unfurled and then began to pass again for Javier, who returned to his senses. He realized that his brother was pretending not to hear their father, and he realized, or sensed, that Mario was going to try to break from his circular path and move away so that the detested voice would be silenced once and for all. Javier shone the light on his brother again, as a warning or a threat, and had to hold back his rage to keep from giving him the beating he'd been ready to give him if Mario didn't do what it took to rescue their father.

He lit up the water again.

The voice cried out. Javier didn't aim the flashlight at his brother this time, since it was clear he'd heard it too and had started turning the boat nearer. The voice became louder, more of this world. Bolts of lightning flashed one after the other, and

Javier spotted his father's head at the crest of a wave. He pointed the light at Mario and saw that he too had seen it, so there was no need to shout or point. The boat took the wave on the diagonal and arced even closer. "Here, over here, assholes!" The lightning flashed and they saw him waving his arms in the water. When it faded, only the beam of the flashlight remained, which now reached their father's position.

Javier grabbed him by the armpits. Mario couldn't and didn't want to help, so his brother had to do it in two stages: first lifting the father till he was hanging halfway into the boat, and then grabbing his legs and lifting him the rest of the way in. When the father tumbled into the boat, Mario sped up and started turning back toward the middle of the gulf. Their father lay on his back for a while in the water at the bottom of the boat, which Javier had started bailing again. Then he sat up.

"You were going to let me drown."

The intensity of the storm was diminishing. Javier had turned off the flashlight and just let time and the movement of the boat go by. He was tired and had lost interest in his father's well-being. If the old man wanted to die, he could go for it. If he was still alive when they arrived – if they arrived – he'd take him to Montería and do everything he could to save him. But if he died anyway, that wouldn't be his problem. Might be best, thought Javier. He'd done his part, and he wouldn't have anything to feel bad about.

The lightning flooded the boat with light, and when everything went dark again, the father asked, "Where are the coolers, you idiots? Where is everything?"

3:00 a.m.

I'm Dairon, the tourist who was drinking aguardiente and doing cocaine behind my wife's back in bungalow four. The thunder was rolling and Gardel the mute was singing. I'd been up drinking still at dawn for the past three nights, while she and my two children slept under the mosquito nets. Every once in a while she'd get up and come in all drowsy and say, "Jesus, Dairon, drinking alone again? You're on your way to becoming an alcoholic. Look at the time."

It must have been because I had the volume turned up really loud, because she always uses earplugs and never usually complains when I put on my music. And after all the time they'd spent in the ocean, nothing could have woken the little ones up.

"I'm going to bed soon. I'll listen to this record and then go to bed. Vacations are about enjoying yourself, right?"

Three claps of thunder boomed out, and she waited with her eyes squeezed shut till they were over. She opened them again very patiently:

"And that's what you call enjoying yourself?"

"Did you see we had to tie the nutbag up?" I asked her to change the subject, but she was already walking away and wanted to sleep, not to hear about tied-up nutbags. I turned down the volume and, once I figured she'd fallen asleep, turned it up again.

I take it easy with the coke, just six lines a night, but it makes it so I don't feel like sleeping much. I use it only on vacation or when things get stressful at the little print shop I've got in Robledo and I have to get rid of a client and clear my head, stuff like that. But hardly ever. I bought a couple of grams off Javier, the owner's son, who's a cool guy. He reads a ton and he likes tango too, but he mostly listens to rock, which I like too, but not for drinking. I listen to Alberto Castillo, Agustín Magaldi, and of course Gardel with my aguardiente, and sometimes Olimpo and Alci Acosta, but mostly tango.

It took four of us to hold her down. The cook's not tiny either, but her husband is this black guy who's like six feet tall – like Foreman, but mean. Everybody says he's just huge and useless, does less work than a weevil on a gravestone and mooches off of her. And he's always dressed nicely – Speedo shorts, flowered shirts, imported sandals. They say he sells weed too. So we managed to get her under control. The other tourist who was helping us, the father of the little girls with the light-colored eyes, the cocky guy with the Toyota – the crazy lady bit him on the arm. So the only skinny people there were the pretty girl who works in the hotel and me. The Toyota guy's got a belly, which is probably a beer gut, because he's a businessman with a lot of money. At least until he gets himself kidnapped – later, alligator.

But we did finally manage to get her tied down. We couldn't call the nurse who lives at a nearby hotel to come give her a shot to calm her down: first, there was that wild storm raging, and plus she wasn't at the hotel, she was off who knows where. All the locals were saying what storm, that wasn't anything, especially compared to the one last year. Well, I said, I wasn't here last year, was I? It was big enough for me! But everybody was worried about the owner and his sons, who'd gone out in that weather and everything. It was already like three thirty. I decided to do one more line and then go to bed, even if I didn't fall asleep. You can't stay up all night all the time, even on vacation. It's hard on the wife and kids to see a father sitting up all night, like Dracula. My wife's patient, I have to say, but you can't take advantage. Antioquian aguardiente is the best. Then she came out again, all disheveled:

"Turn that down a little, would you? Or just go to bed – you need to sleep."

"I'm coming, I'm coming. You're a real pain in the ass, aren't you?" I said.

"So now I'm the pain in the ass! Turn it off and come to bed, Dairon," she said.

At a certain time of night, the best soundtrack is slum tango like Armando Moreno, not that ballroom stuff. *At dawn today I saw her, lonely, ugly, and broken, coming out of a nightclub.*

Now those are lyrics!

And I'm the owner of the Toyota, the father of the little girls with the light-colored eyes. My wife is bandaging my arm where the owner's wife bit me. I bought the SUV for twelve million pesos, and night before last the hotel owner offered me fourteen in cash. I told him I wasn't interested, that just last week in Medellín they'd offered me twenty, also in cash. It's all original, and I added chrome rims and those yellow lights on the roof and bumper. I even added a winch. It's a sweet ride. I'd sell it for twenty-five.

"You can see every single tooth," I said.

"Not every one. Just the ones she has left. It looks like a vampire bite. Hope you don't catch rabies."

The man is always trying to sell me the hotel, and every time we talk, the price goes up ten million pesos. I wouldn't buy a high-end place like the Hotel Nutibara in Medellín at that price. Not even Xanadu, Mandrake the Magician's mansion. The old guy's a good businessman, and he's definitely got dough, but that little hotel isn't worth half of what he thinks it is. Or half of what he's asking, rather, because he's asking for a fortune, and if they give it to him, great, and if not, no problem. There are enough mafia guys around those parts, you never know, and maybe he'll even find a buyer. Maybe he thinks I'm in the mob.

I don't think I'm going to get rabies. That lady put up quite a fight! She gave all of us a run for our money, but I got the worst of it. And all because she tried to hit the fat girl from the kitchen over the head. The hotel's not worth more than a hundred twenty million. The bungalows are falling apart because the sea air eats things up so quickly. Everything but ugly women, ha ha ha. There are lots of sagging doors that don't shut properly, and the tiles in the bathrooms are all chipped and cracked. The kitchenettes are filthy, and the sinks are made of concrete, like for washing mops. The refrigerator is all rusted, and you have to pray to get it to make a couple of ice cubes. Of course the old man doesn't give a crap about that – he doesn't even see those things, or if he does he pretends not to and keeps thinking he's got some kind of palace.

"Shh, the Merthiolate's on its way."

4:00 a.m.

In the flashes of lightning, the father saw that there were no more fish or anything else in the boat. He asked where the coolers were, assholes, the jugs of water, his backpack, but the sons didn't even answer. He remembered falling asleep in the boat and waking up in the water. *Nothing like that's ever happened to me before*, he thought. *Time is really catching up with me. Lucky I'm a hell of a swimmer, or I'd have cramped up and drowned.*

The fever was gone, but he was still weak. He felt nauseated too. It would be best to vomit, clean his body out. He leaned over the side of the boat and retched into the sea with deep heaves that seemed to come from his bones, his very marrow. After a minute he felt better, though he still didn't feel like talking and just stared at the floor of the boat. For some reason, he didn't want to look at his sons.

Javier was bailing in the darkness, and Mario was skillfully guiding the boat through the tall waves. It seemed to the father that the rough seas had grown calmer, or really that they weren't actually rough anymore. Powerful, yes, but nothing to freak out about. The father was hungry, but there was nothing left in the boat. He wanted to ask Javier how far they were from Playamar, but he was stymied by a mounting wave of weakness. *Time gets everybody in the end,* he thought, unable to resist feeling sorry for himself. It occurred to him that he was dying, and he discarded the thought as if shooing a fly away from his face. Sadness overcame him again. Tears pressed against the backs of his eyes like water against a stone dam. Quickly he thought about something else.

He wanted to go to sleep. Two bolts of lightning flashed, tangling together, and lit up the boat, but the father didn't lift his head to see his ungrateful sons. He would have liked for them to ask after his health, his well-being. *It's like they don't give a crap about me,* he thought. And if, at that moment, he'd realized that he was feeling the lack of his sons' affection for the first time in his life, he would have figured he was dying again. He put his arms on his knees and his head on his arms, and the world disappeared.

When he woke up, the darkness and the steady rumble of

the motor were unchanged, and he couldn't tell how long he'd been asleep.

"Are we close?" he asked, but his voice was too weak, maybe, because his sons didn't answer.

I want to sleep, he thought, *I want to go home. I definitely can't count on these losers.*

"Are we close?" he repeated, and didn't get a response this time either. Then he woke up, realized he'd dreamed he was asking, and, now certain of being awake, decided not to ask anything after all. *Begging is the worst thing you can do in life*, he thought. *That's why I've never liked working for anybody, never had a boss, never kneeled down before someone for a few measly pesos. It's cold. My fever's up again. I wasn't born to be a slave. I'd rather die of hunger than serve some other asshole who's actually my equal.*

"We don't have any water, do we? I'm thirsty. What did you turkeys do with all our stuff?"

Silence. The sons either didn't hear or didn't answer.

"What time is it now? Do you think it's almost dawn yet, Javier?"

Again he tricked himself, thinking he was awake when he was actually sleeping. That's why his sons hadn't answered, of course, not because they despised him or were going to toss him overboard again so he'd drown. After a short, intense struggle to wake up, he saw himself again with his head resting on his arms, which were resting on his knees. It was very dark, and he couldn't even see his own feet, which he could tell were submerged in water far above his ankles.

"All right, so nobody's bailing and we're all just going to sink like a bunch of pussies."

"What's the old coot saying now?" asked Mario.

"Be quiet," ordered Javier.

The father wept a little, unsure whether he was awake or asleep, unsure whether his tears were born out of feeling sorry for himself or feeling resentment for his sons. He found it humiliating that Javier now had to defend him to Mario, whom the father had thought of as defective all his life. If he hadn't been so enfeebled, he'd have gone and boxed Mario's ears next to that goddamn motor he claims to know so much about. *Raise crows and they'll pluck out your eyes*, he thought, again awash in self-pity, which surged and ebbed like a tide or a cramp.

He heard his sons talking as if from a great distance.

"Where do you think we are?" Javier was asking.

"We passed the point. We've almost entered the gulf. It's cleared up now. We'll be able to see the lights on the beach soon. Ten minutes and we'll see them."

"Beaching is going to be the hard part. And we have to pull

it off no matter what, so we can find out what's going on with the old man."

"I've landed in rougher seas than this."

He's totally full of himself, the dumb-ass, even though he knows if I were feeling better I'd plunk this boat right down on the sand in front of the hotel. I'm the one who taught them to sail in the first place, and now they're going around like kings, like they've come to my rescue. No way. I'm still the king around here, as the song says. Wait till I get my strength back, dipshits – this old man will show you.

"What's the old bastard saying?"

"Ignore him. He's delirious or something."

Keep quiet, the father told himself when he realized he'd been thinking out loud, *or these two will toss me overboard again. If a man's in rough shape, feeling weak, he has to protect himself like wild animals do when they get sick, where they go off and curl up in a cave somewhere till they get better. Because nobody's going to look after you, no matter how much you've done for them, no matter how much they owe you. No way. They get it in their heads how you're the one who's depended on them and they've achieved everything through their own good looks, and they start thinking of you as a goddamn burden who'd be better off dead. Betrayals like that cut you to your core*, thought the father, tears pressing once more at the backs of his eyes. *Betrayals like that hurt, but they'll be sorry.*

He looked up, and the lights on the shore turned liquid. Feeling sick, he rested his head on his arms again. Javier was still bailing, but the water seemed to keep rising above the father's ankles. He dozed off, and when he woke up he felt better again. The lights he'd seen had definitely been on land. He forgot he'd been about to cry and instead started thinking about getting ashore and the powerful waves that must still be pounding the beach. He felt a stabbing pain in his ankle again, and felt like himself again.

"It's going to be tough," he said, and Javier turned the flashlight on him. "Get that shit off me. Let's be honest, I'm down for the count. Otherwise, I'd take over. Our best bet is for that dumb-ass Mario to give it his best shot, because you're no good at this, as we all know."

Javier didn't say anything.

"What?" the father asked.

"Fine," said Javier.

"If we capsize, we capsize."

"All right, all right, all right."

5:00 a.m.
Mario had calculated they'd reach the hotel a little before daybreak. The waves were still wide and high, but the stars were

out again, and they could see the lights along the beach on the northern end of the gulf. The old man was now telling him what to do, giving him useless orders. Mario had been on the brink of either liberation or perdition, and either would have been welcome. Now he felt sapped by the futile effort and angry at Javier for having thrown their catch overboard, and especially for forcing him to continue living burdened by fate.

We've just got to make it ashore, and what's done is done, Mario thought. The euphoria of imminent danger and defiance helped mitigate his despair. He tried to ignore his father's instructions so they wouldn't piss him off. Mario had seen him in the grip of extreme weakness and vulnerability, the old dolt, but that hadn't restored any of his affection or made his loathing any less corrosive. He recognized the lights of Playamar and saw that there behind it, among the mangroves, the light was starting to dawn. He could also see the foam when the waves crashed and rolled across the water and then across the sand. Without hesitation or consultation, Mario headed the boat toward the beach.

"You have to position yourself on the rear part of the wave and not get up onto the crest," the father said in the darkness, which was now the attenuated darkness of daybreak, and Mario barely managed to hold his tongue and refrain from replying that he already knew what to do, you old bastard. He didn't realize that some of his irritation also came from the fact that his father, when he thought he was teaching them something, used words like *position* instead of *put* and *rear* instead of *back*. And it didn't occur to him that if his father, with a possibly broken ankle and a near drowning only barely behind him, was now being pedantic and overly refined in his speech, it might be because he still wasn't in his right mind.

"Just do your thing. Don't get distracted. Ignore him – he's kind of out of it," said Javier.

Mario waited for the father to lash out at his brother, but it didn't happen. The old man kept staring at the coast as if Javier hadn't spoken.

They were starting to be able to see the outlines of things. The dawn traced the silhouettes of the mangroves and palms. The lights of the hotel, which remained in darkness, were still on. *Our crazy mother must be there*, thought Mario, a little worried, since storms sometimes exacerbated her condition and led to severe crises. Her suicide attempts had taken place on stormy nights, when malevolent creatures flew free on the distraught wind and came from all over like vampires to torment her. Mario was quite familiar with the beings, good and evil, that populated his mother's universe. He knew them better than

Javier, since for a time he'd been able to see them – only every once in a while – though they didn't see him and he wasn't able to talk to them or touch them. And these were things their mother had shared with him, not his brother.

"Once we get near shore, you're going to have to keep the boat moving at the same velocity as the waves. Don't try to go any faster than them, understand?" said the father, and nobody responded. "Did you hear me, asshole?"

"Is there any way to shut him up?" asked Mario.

"All right, keep the speed steady, fine," said Javier.

"And don't let the breakers get ahead of you. If you don't stay on top of these two, they'll screw it all up."

"Jesus Christ!" said Mario.

The father fell silent again as they moved toward the beach. The day kept breaking, generous and varied – in comparison with the night, which was stingy in individual forms yet rich in profundity – but also implacable. Mario had already realized, with some disappointment, that only traces of the rough seas remained and that they'd be able to beach the boat without difficulty. Now he confirmed it. The beach was strewn with branches and bits of trash that had been deposited by the storm surge, and the waves were rolling in, still powerful but now serene.

"Even you would be able to land here," said Mario.

"And pull up the propeller when we touch bottom or you'll ruin the motor, you hear?" said the father.

Three fishermen who'd gotten up early to look at the sea spotted the boat and came to stand in front of the hotel, waiting to help them ashore. Herons flew over Doña Libe and her daughter, who were walking, tiny in the distance, toward the swamp. A bad sign that the mother wasn't with them.

"I have to tell these clowns the same damn thing every single time."

Javier was going to want to rush him to the hospital in Montería so they could take a look at his ankle and see if he'd had a stroke or what, but Mario wasn't about to go anywhere with the old bastard. He planned to drop by to see his mother, get cleaned up, down five or six shots of aguardiente, and sleep twenty-four hours straight. He wasn't even hungry – he just wanted to drink some aguardiente and go to bed. If Javier wanted to deal with the father, that was his business. As far as strokes went, Mario didn't think he'd had one – too bad for them, since they'd have been spared listening to all his bullshit. Hopefully his mother was OK and they wouldn't have to deal with that. The first breaker tried to hurl them forward, but Mario was able to slow the boat down in time so it fell along with the wave. After moving through two more breakers, they reached the most dangerous one, the one that was crashing onto the sand.

"He may not be too bright, but when he learns, he learns," his father said. "Nice job, Mario."

The twin could no longer hear him in the din.

6:00 a.m.

The twins leaped out of the boat. The waves were powerful, and if the fishermen hadn't come to help, they wouldn't have been able to keep the sea from carrying the boat back out, with the father aboard, as the waters ebbed. With the boat beached, the men offered to lift him down, but sitting there on his bench he said no thank you, his sons were more than enough help, and suggested they go inform his wife – Iris, you know? – that he'd arrived.

Javier surveyed the beach, which was strewn with plant debris and trash carried in by the waves. Among the branches and seaweed were empty tin cans, their labels gone. There were soles from men's, women's, and children's shoes. There were toothbrushes and various other kinds of brushes; there were soles from rubber flip-flops. And there was the black Darth Vader helmet, battered by the elements but imposing, perched on a hummock of sand.

Javier climbed into the boat to help the father, whose ankle couldn't have been broken, since otherwise he wouldn't have been able to stand up and lean on his son's shoulder, or lift his foot over the side of the boat and plant it in the sand, grimacing with pain. Mario remained sitting near the water, his elbows on his knees, watching the waves unfurl on the beach. Javier didn't want to call for him to help, since he might refuse.

"If we leave right this minute, we can be at the hospital in an hour and a half," said Javier.

"Hospital? Right this minute? Are you stupid or something? For a sprained ankle?"

"You lost consciousness out there. You almost drowned."

"Because you two idiots were careless. Right? Hang on tight – my foot hurts like hell when I put weight on it."

Javier didn't respond to the carelessness charge. His father might as well have said the sun rises in the west or mangoes fall toward the sky. And though there was no sense in arguing, Javier couldn't help feeling indignant or prevent that indignation from gradually increasing and turning to rage. At that moment, he would have loved to hand the old man off to that bimbo Iris and not have to deal with him again for a long time. If it weren't for his mother and Mario, he'd have told his father and everything else to go to hell and taken off.

Just two months back, he'd turned down a job running a hotel in Cartagena.

Sleepy and half dressed, Iris was waiting for the father, leaning against the door frame on the bungalow porch. She didn't move when they arrived, and Javier had to help his father up the three steps. She didn't move once they were on the porch either. *Is she expecting me to put him to bed too?* thought Javier, and said, "All yours, Iris."

Iris roused herself and hurried to help. The father's weight lifted off Javier's shoulder – the twin felt as if he'd been carrying a load of rocks for twenty-four hours.

"What happened, baby?" Iris asked the father, more out of obligation, Javier thought, than out of real curiosity.

"Nothing. That's what I get for hanging out with losers. Bring me a jug of water with no ice. Help me to the shower – I want to get this salt off me. And tell Imogenia to make me some scrambled eggs."

"Baby, they had to tie Doña Nora up, did you hear? But they've untied her now," said Iris.

"What? The hell with that woman! Such a pain in the ass, goddammit!"

Javier walked back to the boat. Mario was waiting for him so they could go see their mother. The hotel employees were with him, and a few kids were watching. Somebody had handed him a bag of ice to hold against the swelling on his face. Imogenia came walking toward them.

"I know, I know, I know," Javier broke in irritably when Mario started telling him about their mother's breakdown. He was all too familiar with those episodes and didn't have the patience to hear the details right now.

After talking for a minute to the cook, whom Javier had to interrupt to keep her from telling them what had happened, the twins walked in silence to Nora's house. Gardel's timeless voice was issuing from one of the bungalows. *I shouldn't have sold Dairon that coke*, Javier thought. *The moron's never going to go to sleep now.*

"Now the old bastard's saying we were letting him drown out of pure carelessness," said Javier, aware that it was rash to say anything that might revive his brother's resentment for their father.

Mario stood staring at the sand but this time he didn't say anything rude about the father:

"You shouldn't have gone back for him. Things would have been good, Javier."

The grackles were whistling in the palm trees, the herons were traveling their daily route toward the swamp, and a few early-rising tourists were walking along the beach looking at the waves and the debris. Nothing superfluous, nothing lacking. Javier managed to refrain from saying what he was thinking. They'd go fishing with the father on other occasions.

"We'd better take the motor apart and clean it right away," he said instead. "That's all over now, so we can get some sleep, which we could really use at this point."

6:00 a.m. again

The father downed the strong coffee he always drank to start the day and, still limping but without the cane he'd used for almost a month and stopped using two days earlier, went over to Manny's crib, lifted him with his strong, hairy hands, and held the baby in front of his face. Without consulting the doctor, he'd also stopped wearing the annoying ankle brace. The baby smiled. He was a dark cinnamon color, skinny with intense black eyes. He almost never cried. A gorgeous child.

In the bedroom, Iris was sleeping.

Iris snored like a bulldozer, Iris ate a lot, Iris was placid and sensual, Iris was excellent company for a man like him, thought the father. She didn't nag or meddle. She was expert at certain caresses. Sure, she'd gained a little weight from Imogenia's cooking, but her body was even more desirable that way, and she performed those caresses even more expertly, the father thought. Shirtless, in shorts, holding the baby in his muscular right arm, he went out onto the porch and carefully descended the three steps to the sparse grass in front of the house. In the palms, the grackles were whistling, the bitterns gurgling. Limping only slightly, he walked among the bungalows, which were almost all empty now that the high season was over. Waves broke gently at the edge of the glassy sea. He hobbled into the water, and his knotty legs felt the cold, the presence of sardines, happiness. He scooped up water in his hand to wet the boy's head, and the boy did not cry. He kept going till the water was up to his waist, stopped, and submerged the boy little by little. The baby twisted under the water, sleek and firm in his hands, and, when he emerged into the air again, his powerful baptismal wail rang out over the empty beaches.

In the morning the sea mingled with the sun. The father suddenly felt a pang of scorn, love, and compassion for the twins. Some bitterness too, since they were conspiring to mar even that moment. The herons flew over the mangroves, parallel to the beach. *Please, God!* the father asked, almost ordered, in his direct, unsentimental way. *Don't let this one turn out weak like the other two, all right?* Strands of seaweed had been strung out along the sand by the waves, and a few purple jellyfish were gleaming in the first rays of sunlight. Hardly a trace remained of the deluge of chaotic debris that the storm surge had deposited on the beach. Storms, like everything else, are fleeting in their eternity.

archipelago books
is a not-for-profit literary press devoted to
promoting cross-cultural exchange through innovative
classic and contemporary international literature
www.archipelagobooks.org